Richard dreamed he was Fred Astaire and Alfreda, his ex-fiancée, was Ginger Rogers.

He wore black tails and a black bow tie. Alfreda wore a red, quilted horse blanket like the one she'd been lying on in the horse stall. She had four legs. Two of them belonged to her lover.

Richard woke with a jolt. Painfully he went to the bathroom, turned on the cold tap and stuck his head under the faucet for five minutes. Then he filled the tub with warm water, crawled into it and considered drowning himself.

He had to get out of the Gramercy Park house before his grandmother returned. But where would he go? Deportation was the only way he'd ever return to England, which ruled out his mother's London town house. Yesterday, being cut out of his father's will had seemed like a jim-dandy idea, but today he was sober. Sanctuary at his father's farm would be short-lived, since the last place on earth he wanted to be was at Foxglove when dear, old dad came home with a batch of new colts.

For the first time in his life, Richard had no place to run. Oddly, the thought exhilarated him. Captain of his own ship at last, master of his own destiny—and dead broke.

Dear Reader,

What is more appealing, more enduring than *Cinderella, Beauty and the Beast* and *Pygmalion*? Fairy tales and legends are basic human stories, retold in every age, in their own way. Romance stories, at their heart, are the happily ever after of every story we listened to as children.

That was the happy inspiration for our 1993 yearlong Lovers & Legends miniseries. One book each month is a fairy tale retold in sizzling Temptation-style!

The month of July brings the unique voice of Lynn Michaels in her retelling of the *The Ugly Duckling*. Be prepared for more than one surprise along the way!

In the coming months we have stories from bestselling authors including JoAnn Ross, *The Prince and the Showgirl* (*Cinderella*), Bobby Hutchinson, *You Go to My Head* (*The Legend of Bacchus*) and Carla Neggers, *Night Watch* (*Rapunzel*).

We hope you enjoy the magic of Lovers & Legends, plus all the other terrific Temptation novels! Candace Schuler has a fabulous trilogy—Hollywood Dynasty—beginning this month with *The Other Woman*.

Birgit Davis-Todd
Senior Editor

P.S. We love to hear from our readers.

Second Sight

Lynn Michaels

Harlequin Books

TORONTO • NEW YORK • LONDON
AMSTERDAM • PARIS • SYDNEY • HAMBURG
STOCKHOLM • ATHENS • TOKYO • MILAN
MADRID • WARSAW • BUDAPEST • AUCKLAND

To Cathie Linz, who knows everything.
Thanks for the baby steps.

Published July 1993

ISBN 0-373-25549-7

SECOND SIGHT

1

NEW YORK IN NOVEMBER was a dreary damn place to come home to, or so it seemed to Richard Parker-Harris as he paid off a taxi in front of his grandmother's Gramercy Park mansion and gazed up at the dirty snow crusted on the iron grillwork.

Though he doubted he'd find any part of himself still lurking in the bric-a-brac-crammed house, Richard had no place else to go, and so he mounted the front steps with his suitcase. With any luck, his grandmother wouldn't ask about Alfreda. If she'd had her first highball of the day, she might not even remember he had a fiancée.

Ex-fiancée now, Richard reminded himself, as he rang the bell. He wasn't sure what he'd do if his grandmother asked about Alfreda. Go to the Y maybe, or join the merchant marine and get a tattoo. The only thing he knew he wouldn't do was cry. He couldn't remember ever having cried, not once in his whole miserable life.

The door opened and there stood Devlin in his white jacket, shiny black trousers and bow tie. Richard nearly dropped his suitcase. His grandmother's butler looked as though he'd aged twenty years in the past eight.

"Hello, Devlin," he said.

The manservant blinked, then smiled, his face creasing like a piece of old parchment. "Master Richard! What a surprise! Come in, come in do."

Richard stepped past him and put his suitcase down on the terrazzo floor in the foyer. The mahogany paneling on the walls and the staircase smelled like beeswax; the thick, green wool runner on the steps like mothballs.

"Where is she?" Richard asked, surprised to hear himself whisper. His grandmother was the only person allowed to raise her voice in the house. Old habits, he thought ruefully, were hard to break.

"Mrs. Barton-Forbes is not at home." Devlin fastened the last of several locks on the door and gave him a wink. "She and your great-aunt, Agatha, have gone to Lost Wages."

His grandmother's absence drew a relieved laugh from Richard as he shrugged out of his topcoat and handed it over. It was heavy camel hair, and for a moment Richard feared the weight might stagger the old boy, but Devlin managed to wrestle it onto a hanger and tuck it inside the closet beneath the stairs.

"If you'd like to call Madam," he said, as he shut the door, "I have the number of her hotel."

"Let's not spoil her fun," Richard replied. "When do you expect her?"

Devlin gave him a knowing smile as he turned away from the closet. "Madam asked me to meet her with the car at La Guardia at two o'clock on the twenty-fifth. That's three days from now."

Richard smiled back at him. "So it is."

"Your room is ready for you, sir." Devlin's knees cracked as he bent over to pick up the monogrammed leather Pullman. "It always is. Madam insists."

"I know." Richard moved swiftly to intercept him and pick up the case himself. "Is Cook still, uh—"

"Alive?" A dull twinkle lit the old man's cloudy blue eyes. "Yes, sir. Dinner at seven?"

He has cataracts, Richard realized. Devlin has cataracts and still drives the Rolls. Did his grandmother know? Did she even care?

"Seven would be fine. I can find my way up."

"As you wish." Devlin nodded, then added when he reached the landing, "Welcome home, sir."

Gripping the banister in his left hand, Richard looked down at the frail old man who'd taught him how to tie his shoes. "Thank you, Devlin. It's good to be home," he lied, and hurried up the rest of the steps.

He couldn't stay here. Richard knew it before he opened his bedroom door, but the sight of the bed, the spread folded back and the crisp sheets turned down expectantly, clinched it. The last thing his grandmother always said to him whenever he left the Gramercy Park house with a suitcase was, "I'll keep your room ready."

When he'd left for London eight years ago, she'd shrieked it at him as he'd raced out the front door toward the taxi waiting to take him to the airport. He'd sworn to God he'd never come back, yet here he was. It dawned on Richard then that he'd let his grandmother's parting shot hang over him like a curse, dooming him to failure before he even reached the curb.

When things got sticky with his father at Foxglove, Richard Senior's Virginia horse farm, or when he couldn't bear another moment of his mother's indifference during his infrequent visits with her before he'd moved to England, he'd remember his grandmother was keeping his room ready and back he'd come. The question was why the hell it had taken him twenty-nine years to realize it. Maybe he should have a drink and think about it.

Richard knew where his grandmother stashed all her bottles, but went first to the kitchen for ginger ale and ice and a kiss from Cook. She didn't look any older, and Richard felt relieved. If he'd found Cook clumping around the pantry with a walker he might've skipped the Canadian Mist and gone straight to the cooking sherry. Or Bellevue.

Choosing to drink himself senseless in the library, Richard ferreted out the fifth his grandmother kept behind leather-bound volumes of *Tom Jones* and *Paradise Lost*. He'd found his first bottle and his first hangover on the same shelf when he was twelve. So predictable, his Gram.

He mixed himself a highball and downed it in two swallows. It was the first drink he'd had since Alfreda had given his ring back the day before, the umpteenth since he'd found her the day before that, naked and panting, under Phillip Quigley, Viscount Avenel, in one of the horse barns on her father's Surrey estate.

The house party convened by the Earl of Avery to celebrate his daughter's engagement had included Richard's stepfather Sir Freddie, his mother—Lady Simpson since her marriage to Alfreda's second cousin—and at least two dozen other veddy wealthy and veddy proper Britons in addition to Quigley, Richard's nearest rival for Alfreda. None of them had noticed his departure. For all he knew or cared, they were still celebrating Alfreda's engagement. To Quigley now, he was certain.

The barn had been the perfect trysting place, since Alfreda knew Richard hated horses. He'd pretended to tolerate them for her sake, but she'd tumbled when he'd blanched at her suggestion months ago that they make love in her chestnut mare's stall. "There's plenty of room, darling," she'd cooed with glistening eyes. "It's quite a large box. Serena won't even know we're there."

She'd been right about that. The mare had stood docilely in one corner, eyes closed, tail swishing, contentedly chewing bran mash from a nose bag. Richard had stood stricken in the corridor, invisible to horse, man and bitch. Then he'd taken himself up to Lord Avery's Elizabethan manor house and drunk himself silly.

Now he was drinking himself silly in his grandmother's house. What a difference a day made. Maybe he should hop a plane for Vegas. He needed a laugh, and he couldn't think of anything funnier than his grandmother and Aunt Agie at the crap tables.

No, Vegas was a lousy idea. His sinuses were going berserk from eight hours of recycled airplane air, and he shuddered to think of the hot, dry winds that scour the Strip. Rubbing the bump on his nose where Susan Cade, his stepsister Meredith's troglodyte cousin, had broken it with her riding crop some fifteen years ago, Richard decided to have another drink instead.

Four hours and twice as many highballs later, he was sprawled on the leather sofa, his right arm flung over his forehead, the empty Canadian Mist bottle on the floor beside him. Every time he blinked the room swam. At last—he'd drunk himself blind.

Stifling a grin that was mostly yawn, Richard raised his left hand to his eyes. He had a headache and his contacts were killing him. He pressed his thumb and forefinger to his closed lids and froze. His lashes were wet. Heart pounding, he lurched off the couch to the mirror over the fireplace and stared, openmouthed, at the tears brimming in his brown eyes. Were they watering or was he crying?

He'd been thinking about something . . . what was it? Bending an elbow on the mantel, Richard dragged a shaky hand through his tousled blond hair, tried to remember but couldn't. Wasn't this a bitch? He was crying and he was too drunk to think what it was that had moved him to tears.

It wasn't fair. Everybody else in the world cried. Even Alfreda when she'd given back his ring. Why couldn't he?

He thought about his trust fund, most of which he'd pissed away on Lady Alfreda Take-Me-In-A-Horse-Stall-And-I'll-Be-Yours-Forever Simpson. Two hundred grand and six years' salary, every dime he'd earned since he'd graduated from architectural school. Jewelry, clothes, cars, thirty thousand pounds for Serena, the chestnut voyeur. It was enough to make anybody cry, but it only made Richard's tears evaporate, made him realize that he hadn't taken the blow in the heart. He'd taken it squarely in the ego.

The realization hit him like a slap of cold water and cleared some of the whiskey fog clouding his brain. He hadn't been pursuing Alfreda so much as he'd been seeking his father's approval. Since he'd announced the previous spring that he was marrying into one of the oldest equestrian families in England, his frosty relationship with Richard Senior had thawed considerably.

A chip off the old block after all, his father had said. What would the old block say now, Richard wondered, if he knew Alfreda had dumped him because he wouldn't do it in the hay? Let's find out, he decided perversely, turning dry-eyed to the telephone on the desk.

He picked up the receiver, dialed the number at Foxglove and sat in the red leather chair. While he waited for the housekeeper to answer, he decided to tell his father he'd spent every dime of his Barton-Forbes inheritance. Surely Richard Senior would be furious enough to cut him out of his will; surely the thought of supporting himself on his own resources would make him cry.

The housekeeper answered on the fourth ring. "Hello, Mrs. Clark. This is Rich—I mean Tad," he said, using the nickname by which he was known at Foxglove to avoid confusion with Richard Senior. "May I speak with my father?"

"Oh, Taddie! He and Mizzuz Bea left just this mornin' for a yearling sale in Maryland. What a shame! You callin' all the way from London and missin' 'em by a whisker!"

"I'm in New York, Mrs. Clark, at my grandmother's."

"Is Lady Alfreda with you? Did you want to bring her to see the farm? Oh dear! I s'pose I could call—"

"Alfreda isn't with me. She broke our engagement. I've come home for good."

Except I don't know where the hell home is, Richard thought, dragging a hand through his hair again.

"Oh!" she gasped, her soft Southern voice dripping pity. Then she murmured it again, "Ohhh," thoughtfully, and asked, "Did you get your invitation, Taddie?"

"What invitation?"

"Why, your invitation to Miss Meredith's wedding."

"Oh—no." Richard blinked, startled at the news. "I didn't even know she was engaged."

"Oh my, yes. Since she and Miss Susan moved to Santa Barbara. Right after you went to England, Taddie, and Miss Susan graduated vet school. That's why they moved to California, you know. So Miss Meredith and Mister Luke could be together."

"Luke." Richard repeated the name, but it didn't help. "Luke who, Mrs. Clark?"

"You remember Seth Hardin's boy, Taddie. Him an' his daddy used to come out to Foxglove every year for fox hunting season."

"Sort of," Richard hedged, though he hadn't a clue. He'd drunk far too much to remember anything except Susan Cade's dream of becoming an equine veterinarian. Why that should stick in his head he had no idea. "I suppose I should call the little step-brat and congratulate her," he said to Mrs. Clark. "Do you have her number?"

"Sure do. Got a pencil?"

"Yes." Richard bit the cap off a Mont Blanc fountain pen and wrote the area code and number she gave him on the desk blotter. "Thank you, Mrs. Clark. You'll tell my father I called?"

"First chance. Sorry 'bout you and Lady Alfreda, Taddie."

Richard gritted his teeth. He *hated* that nickname. "Thank you, Mrs. Clark."

He hung up and stared, dazed, at the black French telephone. Meredith was getting married. Meredith, the little blond Pan who used to ride her pony hell-bent for leather across the fields and woods of Foxglove Farm. He could hardly believe it, which was ridiculous, since she'd always been every bit as smart and every inch as pretty as her mother, Bea.

Blinking at the phone number he'd scrawled on the desk blotter, Richard reached for the phone, then paused with his hand on the receiver. Tormenting his stepsister—and her dreadful cousin when she'd come to live at Foxglove just a week before she'd broken his nose—had been his favorite adolescent pastime. He'd been damn good at it, too, knew exactly what to do to send Meredith and Susan running and shrieking to his father, but he hadn't seen or talked to either of them in eight years. Maybe if he had another drink he'd remember the right buttons to push.

The closest cache of Canadian Mist was in the music room, in a silver flask under the sheet music in the piano bench. It had sustained Richard through more than one lesson with his Tartar of a piano teacher. As he got up to go get it, the phone rang. He turned back to the desk and answered it.

"Five-five-five—" He started to say the number as was the custom in England, caught himself and said, "Hello?"

"Dickie, what in hell are you doing there?" his mother, Lady Gloria Simpson, demanded imperiously. "Alfreda won't come out of her room, and you've absolutely *ruined* your own engagement party!"

"If the door is locked, then Quigley's with her."

"Beast! A harmless flirtation—"

"She gave my ring back."

"You took it?" His mother sounded incredulous.

"Of course I took it. Then I took myself to Heathrow."

"Dickie, you ass! Let me talk to Mummy. You're drunk."

"So is Mummy by now—" Richard bent his left wrist and peered blearily at his watch "—since it's almost three o'clock in Vegas."

"Whatever is she doing there?"

"Gambling away your inheritance, I hope."

"Oh, dammit, Mummy!" Lady Simpson wailed. "Where are you when I *need* you?"

"Out cold under the blackjack table or I miss my guess."

"Oh my God!" His mother shrieked.

"Don't worry. Aunt Agie won't let them sweep her up with the fallen chips."

"Not Mummy, you idiot! *Alfreda!*" Lady Simpson was screaming now. "I'm on the phone in the game room and the little slut has just this second breezed past the door with Quigley and the Avenel betrothal ring on her finger!"

"Harmless flirtation, eh?"

"Oh *do* shut up, Dickie! I shan't be able to hold my head up after this! *Freddie!*" She shrilled his stepfather's name at C above high C. "How can you even think to congratulate that *selfish* bitch after the insult she's just handed me? The proper thing, my foot! Bring the car round this instant! I won't stay another moment—"

Richard took the receiver away from his ear and depressed the switch hook. His mother was still railing stridently at Freddie when the connection broke.

Dropping the receiver on the desk, he went to the music room for the flask, unscrewed the cap and drank half its contents while he closed the bench and sat at the Steinway grand. He played what tunes he could remember between long, steady pulls, mostly songs he'd learned from Bea.

She'd taught them to him on long, crisp afternoons while Richard Senior and Meredith and Susan—and Seth Hardin's boy, Luke, too, he supposed, though he still couldn't remember him—rode to hounds with the local hunt. Cole Porter and Sammy Cahn stumbled off his fingertips now, but when he was sober Richard played quite well. He had the hands for it, Bea had told him, admiring the full-octave spread he'd been able to make even then.

Sometimes in the evenings when she played for his father, she'd coax him to the piano. The memory of those ghastly recitals superimposed itself on the keyboard and changed Richard's hands. They were no longer the hands of a man, strong, supple and well-manicured, they were the hands of a boy made awkward and clumsy with panic, his nails bitten to the quick.

No matter how well he played, Richard Senior would eventually quit his chair for the hearth rug where Meredith and Susan sprawled on their stomachs, dreaming in soft voices about the horse farm they'd own someday. Richard remembered the fury that used to splotch Bea's face, the chill that hung between her and his father for days afterward.

Part of him always had and, Richard supposed, always would be a little in love with Bea for trying so hard to bridge the gap between him and his father; the rest of him would never forgive her for bringing her niece Susan Cade to Foxglove. Richard was almost fifteen and Susan twelve when she'd come, filthy and uncouth, from some third-rate racetrack in Oklahoma.

Never mind that her drunken horse-trainer father, Loren Cade, had begged Bea to take Susan and "make a lady outta her like her mama was." She'd been resentful as hell and spoiling for the fight Richard had inadvertently given her the morning they'd gone riding with Meredith and he'd used spurs on Valiant, the nasty-tempered old hunter his father insisted he learn to ride.

Richard Senior had given him the spurs as a last-ditch effort to cure Valiant's habit of swinging his head around and nipping Richard's knees. Susan hadn't known that, of course, she'd simply gone nuts and hit Richard with her riding crop when he'd raked Valiant's flanks. Hard enough to unseat him and smash his nose all over his face. Valiant had trotted happily home to his stall. Richard had returned reeling and bleeding and clinging to the back of Meredith's saddle.

"A *girl!*" His father had roared at him all the way to the local hospital's emergency room. "A goddamn *girl* breaks your goddamn nose and you goddamn *let* her!"

The next day Richard had taken himself and his nose splint back to New York. Back to the cold, bitter house in Gramercy Park where he now sprawled on the piano bench, passed out with his right arm bent above the keyboard, his head buried in the crook of his elbow.

When he began to snore, a single tear dripped out of his left eye and splashed on the black-and-white ivories.

2

A HALF SECOND before her hand closed on the stall door, the piano music playing mindlessly and mostly off-key inside Dr. Susan Cade's head stopped. In a jarring minor chord, as if invisible fingers had slipped clumsily off the keys. So abruptly that her hand jerked back from the latch.

Screwy, Susan thought, but at least it had stopped. Every bit as suddenly as it had started, about twenty minutes ago as she'd climbed behind the wheel of her Chevy Blazer to make the drive to Roundhouse Stables. Not a moment too soon, either, since even on days when he wasn't doing his best to live up to his name, Satan was a handful.

"Chickened out, huh?" Luke Hardin bent his elbows on the stall door and grinned. "At last you admit defeat."

"Fat chance." Susan grinned back at him and reached for the latch, the last strident echo of the music fading away inside her head. "The day I let Satan put one over on me is the day I burn my vet school diploma."

At the sound of his name, Satan raised his black head and snorted. Age had speckled his muzzle with gray, but no one, not even Luke who'd inherited Roundhouse from his father, knew exactly how old the gelding was. Judging by his teeth, Susan figured he was about seventeen. When she lifted the latch, Satan flattened his ears.

"I dunno, Suz." Luke straightened and opened the half door for her. "Today could be the day."

"You wish," she said, sliding past him into the stall.

Luke pushed the door shut with a click. "Wanna bet?"

Tucking her hands in her back pockets, Susan faced him and smiled, her chin-length auburn hair gleaming in a dusty shaft of midafternoon sun slanting through the window beneath the eaves. "Make it easy on yourself."

"A buck and a half."

"Ooh, big spender. That's all you're willing to bet I can't get out whatever's stuck in Satan's hoof?"

"Nope." Luke fished a stopwatch out of the front pocket of his faded jeans and waggled his sandy eyebrows at her. "I bet you can't do it in five minutes."

"Well, if you're going to make it difficult." Susan folded her arms and smiled. "Bet me High Brow."

At the sound of her name, the two-year-old chestnut filly swung her white-blazed head inquiringly over the door of her temporary stall across the row. The sight of her delicately pricked ears and dished muzzle made Susan's mouth water.

"Not in a million years and you damn well know it," Luke replied with a grin. "But I admire your tenacity, Suz, and Meredith's. She's still trying to sweet-talk me into giving her High Brow as a wedding present."

"She'd better hurry. Only thirty-one more shopping days left till Christmas and your wedding."

"Don't remind me. Buck and a half, Suz. Take it or leave it."

"Easy money, Hardin. You're on."

Susan turned toward Satan. The gelding snorted and fixed a gleaming black eye on her, his left rear hoof held gingerly above the straw.

"You got guts, Doc," said Paulie O'Gilbert, the stable boy, perched on High Brow's stall. "I wouldn't go back in there for a hundred and fifty bucks."

The gauze patch taped to the slight eighteen-year-old's bicep said why. The nasty bite beneath was the thanks Satan had given him when he'd tried to check his sore hoof.

"How're you going to ride High Brow and the other monsters around here," Susan asked over her shoulder of the boy who aspired to be a jockey, "if you let a Shetland pony get the best of you?"

"Satan," Luke said, "has the soul of Attila the Hun."

"And teeth like a great white shark," Paulie added, his face flaming with embarrassment.

"Yeah, teeth like a shark." Luke gave Susan a wink Paulie couldn't see. "If Satan didn't keep High Brow cool, calm and collected, I'd grind him up for dog food."

Which he would never do, Susan knew, since Luke was as devoted to Satan as the old pony was to High Brow. The tough little Shetland had been stablemate and stabilizer to at least four generations of high-strung Roundhouse Thoroughbreds. Love, not fear, had prompted Luke to call her on a Sunday afternoon, but the lie squared Paulie's shoulders and diffused some of the red staining his cheeks.

"No offense, Paulie." Susan smiled at the boy. "I keep forgetting you can't talk to horses like I can."

The stable boy grinned. "Yeah right, Doc."

"But Paulie," Susan insisted, her violet eyes twinkling, "I really *can* talk to horses."

"Hey Doc, I believe you," Paulie said, shaking his leg as if she were pulling it.

"Just watch, skeptic." Susan turned back to the pony. "Satan and I understand each other. Don't we, Satan?"

The pony eyed her balefully.

"Are you tired of standing on three legs yet?"

Satan flattened his ears, shook his head and snorted.

"Baloney." Susan waded purposefully through ankle-deep straw. "It does too hurt, you old crank."

As she approached, Satan turned his head to keep her in view and rumbled at her from deep in his chest.

"Oh yeah?" Susan laid the first two fingers of her left hand on his muzzle. "Bite me and I'll bite you back."

"I love it when she does this." Paulie jumped down from High Brow's stall, crossed the corridor and folded his arms on the door beside Luke. "She makes it look like she really is talking to him."

Shifting his weight onto his left elbow, Luke glanced sideways at the boy. "How do you know she isn't?"

"Give it a rest, boss." Paulie rolled his eyes and turned to watch Susan.

Luke just smiled and did the same.

Susan smoothed her hand down the pony's short neck and along his back to his rear quarters, feeling the muscles jump beneath his shaggy hide. Poor thing really was in pain.

"There's no fool like an old fool, Satan." Susan ran her hand slowly down his left rear leg to check for inflammation in the tendons. "If you'd let Paulie do this, you wouldn't have had to stand around hurting all this time."

The pony snorted and began to tremble, but otherwise stood quietly. Bending from the waist, Susan cupped his hoof in her hands to examine it.

From the stall door the view of her long, shapely legs and the well-worn denim encasing them stretched to its limits was spectacular. When she reached for the hoof pick in her back pocket, Luke gallantly averted his gaze, unfortunately in Paulie's direction. Arm bent on the top of the door and fist pressed to his cheek, Paulie gazed at Susan with a silly, slack-jawed grin on his face.

"This is the part I *really* love," he murmured.

The poke Luke gave him in the ribs knocked his elbow out from under him. "Go cool yourself out."

"You get to watch," Paulie complained, swiping his carroty hair off his forehead.

Luke smiled. "I'm the boss."

He looked back at Susan in time to see her drop to her heels. Sliding her hands down Satan's leg, she eased his hoof to the straw and straightened. The pony shifted his weight and snorted, his ears springing up as if in surprise.

"Here's the problem." Susan tucked the hoof pick in her pocket, gave Satan a reassuring slap and started toward Luke and Paulie with a thin aluminum ring winking on her raised index finger. "Pop top from a soda can."

Behind her, the old pony laid back his ears and bared his teeth. Luke opened his mouth to warn her, but she'd already spun around and clamped her hand on his left ear. The pinch of her slim but strong fingers forced Satan's head to the side and made it impossible for him to bite.

"Mind your manners." Susan wagged the pop top under his muzzle. "Or I'll put this back where I found it."

She squeezed his ear again to let him know she meant it, then released him. With an indignant snort, Satan swung away from her and tugged a mouthful of hay from the overhead rack.

"That's all you have to do, Paulie," Susan said, as she left the stall. "Just let him know who's boss."

"Looks easy when you do it," he replied just a bit testily, as he swiped his long bang of orange hair over the chevrons shaved in his scalp above his pierced left ear. "Want me to put High Brow back in with Satan, boss?"

"Okay, Doc?"

"Sure." Susan crossed the row and cupped her palm over High Brow's nose. The filly whickered, fluttering her velvety nostrils beneath her fingers. "Let her see for herself that Satan's okay."

Lifting her sheepskin-lined denim jacket from the door of an adjacent stall where she'd tossed it, Susan moved out of the way with Luke while Paulie moved the chestnut filly across the corridor to the roomy box she shared with Satan. The reunion between sleek, long-legged High Brow and the fat, shaggy pony was brief and touching. Soft nickers, fluttered nostrils, then High Brow turned her nose to her grain box, her supple neck arched protectively over Satan while the pony continued to pull hay from the rack.

"Cute, aren't they?" Luke took Susan's elbow and drew her away from the stall.

"Darling," she replied, sliding him a smile as they walked up the row. "They remind me of you and Meredith."

"Funny, Suz." Luke smirked at her. "Real funny."

Susan laughed and slung her jacket over her shoulder. The sound of her voice drew the attention of the occupants of the stalls they passed. Elegant equine heads appeared, swinging over half doors in her direction. Ears pricked and nostrils fluttering, Susan's patients stretched their necks for a pat or a scratch.

"I wonder how Paulie would react," Luke said thoughtfully, as she stopped to stroke a bay gelding named Knockdown, "if he knew you really could talk to horses."

"Not funny," Susan warned over her shoulder. "He'd probably start wearing a garlic clove earring."

"Look nice with his haircut."

Luke grinned, but Susan's frown deepened, causing Knockdown to snort and swing his head away.

"Sorry, fella." She gave the bay an apologetic pat, and Luke a sharp, sidelong look and started up the row again.

"Don't worry, Suz," he said, catching up with her in two strides, "I'm not going to tell Paulie."

"I wouldn't mind," she replied, shrugging into her jacket as they neared the far end of the barn, "if people didn't look at me like I was some kind of freak."

"Says who?" Luke reached ahead of her to open and hold the door. "I don't think you're a freak."

"That's because Meredith told you." Susan turned sideways to face him and slide through the door. "You'd believe anything that came out of her perfect, bow-shaped lips."

"True," Luke granted good-naturedly, following her outside and letting the door fall shut behind them with a whap. "But it explains a lot of things I've seen you do. Like lay your hand on the muzzle of a horse half-crazy with pain and it stops thrashing and kicking. Nobody else can do that."

Shrugging, Susan shoved her hands in her pockets and shivered. The afternoon was partially overcast, the sun a silver disk behind a thin screen of gray clouds, but it wasn't cold. It only seemed chilly after spending time in the barn and the heat radiated by the stabled horses. A ripe kind of warmth to some, but to Susan the smell of horse and hay and manure was the smell of comfort and belonging.

"That's the plus side of being telepathic," she said, squinting at the sky and wondering if it would rain. "The downside is doing the very thing you described and having somebody look at you like you just did voodoo."

"So why do you kid about it like you do with Paulie?"

"It's like being born with a really big nose." Susan fished her keys out of her right pocket as they approached her blue-and-silver Blazer parked in the small paved area next to the barn. "If you point it out and joke about it, people don't seem to notice it as much."

She'd washed the truck that morning. If it rained she'd have to wash it again. Too bad her telepathy only worked with horses. Too bad she couldn't forecast the weather.

"I'm glad you can't read *my* mind." Luke opened and held her door. "I'd have no secrets at all from Meredith."

"You've got damn few as it is." Susan got in behind the wheel and stuck the key in the ignition. "Course I could make a fortune collecting hush money from you."

"Scary thought. Which reminds me." Luke pushed the door shut, rested one hand on the rolled-down window, and dug a crumpled dollar bill and two quarters from his pocket with the other. "A buck and a half, right?"

"Right." Susan took the money with a smug smile. "Someday you may learn *not* to put your money where your mouth is. At least with me."

"Gambling's in my blood. It's why I own racehorses."

"You're in the right line of work."

"So are you. Except for one teensy little problem."

"What's that?" Susan asked, as she started the engine.

Luke grinned and backed away from the truck. "The only studs in your life have four legs, a mane and a tail."

He laughed heartily, but Susan gave him a puckered, we-are-not-amused smile. "Very funny," she said. "See you tomorrow on rounds, Mr. Comedy."

Susan backed the truck out of its space and turned onto the road. In the rearview mirror, she saw Luke making his way back to the barn with his hands in his pockets, and laughed as she rolled up the window.

She'd have to come up with something really evil to get him back. Wasn't much time. Wasn't much fresh material either, since she and Luke had been heckling each other unmercifully from her first day as Roundhouse vet. That was almost three years of nonstop ribbing; thirteen if she counted from the first time she'd met him at Foxglove.

Which Susan didn't do very often, since it reminded her of things not quite so pleasant as how starry-eyed Luke and Meredith had been about each other even as gawky, goofy fourteen-year-olds. Susan had been fourteen, too, when Luke had come with his father to visit his old friend Uncle Richard, just as gawky and just as goofy, too. About a boy who was now a man and engaged to Lady Alfreda Something-Or-Other.

"So Luke," Susan murmured as she drove slowly past white rail fences toward the nearest of Roundhouse's several exits, "does Meredith stand on a box to kiss you or do you get down on your knees?"

Pretty old, but it might work. Susan drummed her fingers on the wheel, grinning suddenly as the truck neared the gate and she stepped on the brake and the clutch. Does Meredith stand on a mounting block was even better. Great double entendre.

"Heh, heh, heh." Susan waggled her eyebrows at her reflection in the rearview mirror, wrapped her arms around the top of the wheel and leaned forward to check the traffic before pulling out onto the two-lane county blacktop.

While she waited for a grain truck to rumble past, the jingle of her keys against the steering column snagged her attention. The faint ting-ting-ting reminded her of a child's toy piano and the music she'd heard earlier inside her head.

Where the heck had it come from? Susan wondered, lifting her right hand from the wheel to catch the keys in her fingers. Maybe Meredith, she thought, rubbing her thumb across the onyx horse head stamped on the silver key tag.

If her cousin concentrated hard enough, Susan could sometimes pick up a stray thought or two. And God knew, as badly as Meredith played her grandmother's cherry spinet, it would take phenomenal concentration just to get her through "Chopsticks."

No, the music had been too sophisticated for Meredith. Shaking her head perplexedly, Susan started her left turn onto the highway. Bea played well enough, but Susan had never picked up anything from anyone else in the Parker-Harris family except—

The identity of the phantom pianist hit her so suddenly she jammed on the brake and the clutch and skidded the truck to a halt in the middle of the fortuitously empty highway. Hands clamped on the wheel, her keys swinging and jangling madly from the ignition, Susan stared wide-eyed and straight ahead as the disjointed piano music welled out of her memory in broken chords and clumsy runs.

"Oh no," she breathed, a shiver of recognition crawling up her back. "Oh *Richard*."

When he was sober he played like Rachmaninoff. Susan had listened to him play often enough at Foxglove to know—mostly in the evening while she sprawled, chin in hand in front of the fire with Meredith and Uncle Richard. A few times while he practiced in the afternoon, she had listened from the staircase where he couldn't see her, one arm wrapped around the newel post wishing she'd never broken his nose.

He'd never forgiven her for making him look like a wuss in front of his father, and Susan knew he never would. Just like she knew something was wrong, very wrong. She read Richard's pain as clearly as she always had, felt it like she felt distress in a horse, in a slow, half-sick prickle across the nape of her neck.

Taking a deep breath to still her pounding heart, Susan eased off the brake and sped home at ten miles above the limit. Meredith was the worst, the absolute last person she should tell this to, but she had to tell someone. Long ago she'd learned if she didn't, she'd explode.

On that score at least she was one up on Richard.

3

RICHARD DREAMED he was Fred Astaire and Alfreda was Ginger Rogers. He wore black tails and a black bow tie. Alfreda wore a quilted red horse blanket like the one she'd been lying on in Serena's stall. She had four legs. Two of them belonged to Phillip Quigley.

He woke with a start, facedown in bed, mouth open, head thudding, blinded by the blazing light flooding the room. Cursing the idiot who'd left the lamps on, Richard stuffed the pillow over his head. When he dared to lift one corner and crack an eyelid, he realized the glare was cold November sunshine pouring through the window on the far wall. He also realized, since he could see the window, that he was still wearing his contacts.

Without trying, he knew standing was out of the question, so he did what he'd seen his grandmother do more than once. He eased out of bed on his hands and knees and crawled to the bathroom across the hall.

His arms and legs were bare, which meant whoever had hauled him upstairs had also undressed him. He hoped it was Devlin, since Alfreda had selected his very brief navy briefs. Now that he was a free man he could throw them the hell away and buy decent white underwear.

Gritting his teeth, Richard leaned over the icy side of the bathtub, turned on the cold tap and stuck his head under the faucet for a good five minutes. Then he filled the tub with warm water, crawled into it and considered drowning himself. He was still considering it when Devlin appeared with a mug and a thermal carafe in one hand and a glass of something that looked like—but Richard was willing to bet wasn't—strong iced tea.

"Madam swears by this, sir," Devlin said.

"What is it?"

"It goes down better if you don't know."

The concoction wasn't steaming, yet bubbled slowly like a geyser. Richard's stomach heaved. "No thanks," he said, sinking up to his chin in cooling water.

"Madam telephoned this morning to say she's coming home today. I'm to meet her flight at five-forty."

Like a whale breaking the surface, Richard surged out of the water and grabbed the glass so suddenly that a small tidal wave gushed over the side and splashed Devlin's spit-polished black shoes. Holding his breath, Richard drank, gasped and shuddered, then croaked, "What time is it?"

"Quarter past nine." Devlin filled the mug and gave it to him. "Would you like your dressing gown?"

"Please." Richard gulped coffee while Devlin went for his robe. When he came back he asked, "Did my mother ring?"

"Late last evening on the house phone, sir. She asked the number of Madam's hotel and told me to check Madam's private line. I found the library extension off the hook."

Uh-huh, Richard thought darkly. "I'll be down shortly." He emptied the mug and gave it to Devlin, his stomach settled, the pounding in his head receding. "Would you ask Cook for a poached egg and dry toast?"

"Certainly, sir." The butler took the cup, picked up the empty glass and left.

Five-forty gave Richard eight hours max to remove himself from the Gramercy Park house before his grandmother returned. Remove himself to where was the burning question, and at the moment he hadn't a clue. He did have a relatively clear head, thanks to Devlin's potion. He put it to the problem while he drained the tub, turned on the shower, soaped and rinsed himself and washed his hair.

Deportation was the only way he'd ever return to England, which ruled out his mother and Freddie's London town house. Yesterday, being cut out of his father's will had seemed like a jim-dandy idea, but today he was sober. Sanctuary at Foxglove would be short-lived in any case, since the last place on earth he wanted to be was his father's farm when he came home with a batch of new colts.

For the first time in his life, Richard had no place to run. Oddly, the thought exhilarated him. Captain of his own ship at last, master of his own destiny—and dead broke. What price freedom, he thought ruefully, as he stepped out of the tub and into his robe, tugged a towel off the bar and dried his hair.

He'd been many things in his life but never poor, and he supposed he really wasn't now, since he did have a profession, a few thousand in bonds due to mature in three months, a couple grand left on his bank card, and of course, American Express. Poverty was a relative concept, Richard reflected, and he was just beginning to realize there were things in life far worse than being without money.

Tops on the list was waking up after a roaring drunk to discover you're almost thirty years old and don't know who the hell you are or what the hell you want. The realization hit Richard as he walked across the hall ruffling the towel through his hair, and brought him into a dead stop in the middle of his bedroom.

The shrill ring of the telephone jarred him out of his daze. He answered it on the third ring with a curt, "Hello?"

"Don't you *dare* hang up on me, Dickie!" his mother said.

Dickie, Richard, Tad, he thought irritably, yanking the towel off his head. Was it any wonder he didn't know who he was? Nobody else did, either. "You were so busy screeching at Freddie, I didn't think you'd notice I'd rung off."

"I do *not* screech!" his mother screeched.

"Please." Richard sank on the edge of the bed and pinched the bridge of his nose. "My head."

"You drink too much. Don't think I haven't noticed."

"So does Mummy. Where do you think I learned it?"

"It's the reason Alfreda broke it off with you," she went on, ignoring his comment. "She told me, you know."

"Remind her that it's a lot easier to cuckold a drunk."

"Alfreda and I had quite an interesting chat last night after the *dreadful* row she had with Quigley," Lady Simpson announced archly. "Would you like to hear about it?"

"No."

"She's willing to take you back."

"I don't want her."

"Don't be a fool, Dickie! Think of the circles you'll move in, the advantages of being Lord Avery's son-in-law."

"All of which will be *yours*, as well."

"Well, naturally, darling."

"Then divorce Freddie and marry her yourself. I don't want Alfreda. I never wanted Alfreda. I wanted to impress my father. I realized that yesterday."

"*Your father!* Why should the opinion of a man to whom you've never been anything but a disappointment matter to you?"

"I don't know why. I don't know what I want, either, except white underwear."

"You've been drinking again, haven't you?"

"No. I've come out of my stupor. I don't mean the one I was in yesterday, I mean the one I've been in my whole damn life. I've no idea what brought me out of it. Maybe the shock of seeing how Devlin has aged. Did you know he taught me to tie my shoes?"

"How nice. Now listen closely, Dickie, Mummy and I have it all worked out. You'll have to buy Alfreda a present, of course—"

"Oh, of course." Richard tucked the receiver between his shoulder and his tightening jaw, folded his arms and listened, grimly fascinated to hear just how far she'd go.

"Something expensive and frivolous," Lady Simpson went on, completely missing the sarcasm in his voice. "Mummy will go with you to Tiffany's tomorrow. And wire flowers to Alfreda's London flat. She'll be driving back with Freddie and me in the morning.

"Then get yourself on a late evening flight, which will put you into Heathrow in plenty of time to come by the house for lunch. We'll invite Alfreda. And Lady Avery, too, so pick up something for her as well, Dickie, and don't forget to shave on the plane. Oh! And be sure to take your antihistamine."

"My nose! You remember!" Richard exclaimed, surprised and momentarily disarmed by her uncharacteristic concern.

"Well *of course* I remember. The vulgar snorting and blowing you go through if you forget to take your antihistamine is quite unforgettable. I don't know why you don't see a specialist."

"I *did*." Richard's clenched jaw began to twitch as he unfolded his arms and gripped the receiver in his right hand. "Fifteen years ago when Meredith's cousin Susan broke it. You do remember my stepsister, Meredith, don't you? Dad adopted her when he married Bea because I've always been such a disappointment to him!"

"Why are you shouting about that dull woman's child?" his mother demanded petulantly. "And why are you shouting at *me?* For heaven's sake, Dickie, I can't be expected to remember *everything!*"

And then she burst into tears, her oldest and best trick to punish him and make him feel like slime. Pliant slime so overcome with guilt that he'd do whatever she asked if only she'd forgive him and promise not to cry anymore. Why did he see it so clearly now? Why hadn't he years ago?

"You could at least remember my name," he told her bitterly. "It's Richard."

"That's *his* name!" Lady Simpson wailed. "I can't call you by *his* name. Dickie suits you so much better."

"It doesn't suit me at all. Nor does returning to England to marry Lord Avery's kinky daughter so you can move up a rung on the social ladder. You might as well call Mummy and tell her to stay loaded and stay in Vegas, because I'm not going to be here this afternoon so she can badger and bully me. Those days are gone and so am I!"

Richard slammed the phone down and sat with his hand on it, his chest heaving, his head pounding. That was his mother's second-best tactic. When the going got rough, she called in the cavalry, his tough-as-Cook's-hard-rolls old Gram, the only one allowed to raise her voice in the Gramercy Park house. Only a fool would dare argue with a perpetually half-lit old harridan.

The phone rang, shrill and sharp beneath Richard's hand. He grasped the wire connecting it to the wall and yanked, hard enough to rip the jack out of the wall and smack himself in the nose with it. He saw stars and fell back on the bed.

"Dammit to hell!" he shouted, wincing as he touched his throbbing proboscis.

His nose hadn't taken a sharp left toward his ear, it just felt like it had. That was a relief, but Devlin's appearance in the doorway did not improve his temper. It meant the faint ringing he'd heard wasn't inside his head.

"Master Richard," Devlin said, "your sister, Miss Meredith, is waiting on the house phone to speak to you."

"Meredith?" Richard wheeled off the bed, the bridge of his nose pulsing with every beat of his heart.

He'd expected Devlin to say his mother or his grandmother was on the other line. Had he phoned Meredith yesterday? He couldn't remember.

"She's calling long-distance, sir," Devlin said, eyeing the jack still swinging from the cord in his hand.

Mrs. Clark had told him Meredith was—somewhere. Hell. He couldn't remember. "Did she say from where?" Richard gave the jack a backhand toss and started through the doorway as Devlin stepped out of his way.

"No sir," Devlin replied, trailing him along the hall and down the stairs, "but she lives in Santa Barbara now."

That was it, California, but that's all he could recall. "Since when?" Richard asked, turning on the landing and looking back at Devlin following carefully with his hand on the banister.

"I believe she and Miss Susan bought their ranch just after you left for England, sir."

Coincidence, maybe, but Richard didn't think so, anymore than he thought it coincidence for Meredith to call. He couldn't remember passing out, but he remembered Mrs. Clark's thoughtful "Ohhh," and felt the first stirring of suspicion as he hurried along the ground-floor passageway that led to the kitchen and the butler's pantry.

There he found the receiver of the house extension lying on its side in the middle of the rolltop desk where Devlin kept the household accounts. He also found a pair of glasses with lenses so thick they crossed his eyes when he picked them up. He set them aside, felt the balloon that swelled in his chest at times of stress inflate, picked up the phone and asked, "Did you call Mrs. Clark or did she call you?"

"She called me," his stepsister replied without hesitation. "Welcome home, big brother. Long time no see."

"Thanks very much, Merry. Now what the hell d'you want?"

"Got smashed last night, didn't you?"

Meredith's perception over thousands of miles and an eight-year absence sent a wave of heat shooting through Richard. It took him a minute to realize he was blushing. He hadn't since he was fifteen.

"Ever hear of jet lag?"

"Ever hear of the Betty Ford Clinic? It saved Uncle Loren's life."

"Dried out, has he?"

"Completely. You should try it."

Richard felt himself flush again and wondered what was wrong with him. Maybe Devlin's potion.

"Mrs. Clark told me you hadn't received your invitation," Meredith said, "so I'm calling to invite you to my wedding."

"Oh—yes. Congratulations."

"Thank you. I want the whole family here, Richard. I won't take no for an answer."

"I've no intention of saying no, Meredith. I'd be delighted to come. When is the happy day?"

"Christmas Eve. Pretty sappy, huh?"

Sappy as hell, Richard thought, but lied and said, "Not at all. I think it's charming."

"So when can you come?"

"When do you want me?"

"As soon as possible."

"Why?" Richard asked sharply, his suspicions resurfacing.

"I'm up to my neck in lace and tulle and RSVPs, that's why. I could use an extra pair of hands."

"Why doesn't Susan help you? Or does she still sign her name with an *x*?"

"She doesn't have time. She has the ranch to run, plus she's staff vet at Roundhouse."

"Roundhouse what?"

"Roundhouse Stables. Luke's place."

"Luke who?"

"Luke Hardin," Meredith said testily. "My fiancé."

"Seth Hardin's boy," Richard replied, the one he still couldn't remember. "Why don't you hire a secretary?"

"All right, Richard," Meredith said with a sigh. "Want me to cut to the chase?"

"Please," he replied, sitting on a corner of the desk.

"Here's how I see it. One day you're in England with a titled fiancée, the next you're in New York with a hangover. Mrs. Clark told me you got dumped, but considering the haste of your departure I'd say there's more to it than that. I'm not asking what, I'll wheedle it out of you later. Devlin told me your grandmother's coming home this afternoon. Quite suddenly, he said, three days earlier than planned. If I were you, I'd want to clear out of there before she arrives. How am I doing so far?"

"Very well," Richard replied, torn between chagrin and admiration. How was it Meredith knew so much about him, while he could do little more than recall that her eyes were blue? "Keep going."

"I could honestly use your help and you obviously need a place to hide out. I'm offering you one in the last place on earth your grandmother would ever think to look for you—a horse farm in California."

"What an amazingly perceptive little step-brat you've grown up to be, Meredith. You're absolutely right. A horse farm in California is positively the last—" Richard sat bolt upright on the desk corner. "Wait a minute—" Devlin had said something about a ranch, too. "What horse farm in California?"

"Good heavens, Richard. How many brain cells did you kill last night?"

"Not that many. I've been out of the country for eight years, if you'll recall."

"Mother wrote you religiously every week. Even I dropped you a line now and then. Didn't you read our letters?"

"Well, I—"

"Oh, never mind," Meredith spat disgustedly. "Cicada Ranch, Richard, is the horse farm you told Susan and me we'd never have. It's our very own little four-hundred-acre pipe dream outside Santa Barbara."

Bits and pieces of Bea's letters, the ones Richard read hastily and never answered, were coming back to him now. So was the slow, half-sick churning he'd wakened with in his stomach.

"You mean you did it? You actually managed it?"

"Of course we did. We said we would."

"But how? Did you rob a bank?"

"Of course not. Think about it. It'll give you something to do on the plane besides drink."

"Very funny, Meredith."

"So how about it? Will you come?"

"Yes, I'll come. Where are you exactly and how do I get there?"

"Taken care of. I've booked a seat for you on the one-o'clock nonstop out of La Guardia. Can you make it?"

Richard glanced at the clock on the wall, the big round one with oversize numbers and bright red, easy-to-see hands. It was quarter past ten. "Just," he said.

"Got a pencil?"

"Yes." Richard plucked a freshly sharpened one from the World's Greatest Dad mug he'd given Devlin for Christmas the year he was seven, tore a page off a memo pad and wrote down the flight number, the address and instructions to pick up the rental car Meredith had reserved for him.

"One more thing, in case you're wondering," she said. "Cicada is big enough that you'll never have to see Susan unless you want to. Except at dinner and at the wedding, of course."

That gave Richard a shock, since he was just thinking more or less the same thing himself. "Very thoughtful of you, Merry, but I've quite outgrown that adolescent silliness."

"That's what Susan says," Meredith replied with a laugh, "but I don't believe her, either. Bye now."

Richard hung up the phone and stared at it, wondering. Meredith's invitation was too good to be true, which meant it probably was. A gift horse of similar proportions had sunk the Trojans, but Richard decided not to look this one in the mouth. He didn't have the time—and he had no other choice. Instead he picked up the phone to dial a taxi, then changed his mind and hung up.

He'd drive Devlin to La Guardia in the Rolls. That way he'd make sure the old boy got there in one piece.

4

ON THE PLANE Richard nursed a Bloody Mary and tried to figure out how Meredith and Susan had amassed the fortune four hundred acres of real estate in the posh environs of Santa Barbara must have cost them. It came to him in a blinding flash of memory, not vodka, somewhere over the Midwestern prairies.

So did a plan for recouping his trust fund. A plan so brilliant it brought a grin to his face and a stewardess to his seat. Trading the dregs of his drink for black coffee, Richard sipped it gratefully and thanked God he hadn't killed all the cells in his brain.

Fifteen years ago he hadn't believed Meredith when she'd come to his room the day after Susan broke his nose to help him pack and tell him why she'd done it. It had taken the annual family trip to Churchill Downs for the Kentucky Derby the following May to convince him. He'd watched his father diligently study his racing form, carefully place wagers based on breeding, past performance and times and lose his shirt. Then he'd watched Meredith and Susan hang together, whispering over the paddock rail as the horses paraded before each race, then give their money and instructions for placing their bets to Bea. They'd made eight thousand, four hundred and sixteen dollars on that particular Derby day.

After that, Richard had no problem believing Susan Cade was telepathic, that she could read equine minds and not only feel their pain—as she'd done when he'd spurred

Valiant—but deduce from watching them prance and dance in the post parade which ones were at their peak and most likely to win. He'd never taken advantage of Susan's gift before, but he'd never been broke before. She'd never apologized for breaking his nose, either. An afternoon at the track, he decided, was the perfect way for Susan to say she was sorry.

Devising the plan eased some of the guilt Richard felt at abandoning Devlin. Once the plane landed, the beauty of the little Eden God made and the Spanish named Santa Barbara took care of the rest.

He was damn grateful for the Spaniards, who'd arrived ahead of the L.A. real estate developers and left their elegant mark on the land. The names they'd bequeathed— the Santa Ynez Valley, Isla Vista, San Marco Pass—made Richard smile as he stood in line at the car rental booth reading a road map.

He left the airport in a Ford Tempo, feeling like Mohammed entering Mecca for the first time. He'd studied world-famous examples of Spanish architecture, but had never seen a place where they fit so perfectly, where they actually seemed to be a part of the landscape. Well, maybe Seville.

He also found a climate that didn't send his sinuses into spasms. Driving around rubber-necking with his window down, he drew his first deep breath in years. It was all the proof he needed that at last Dickie/Tad/Richard had found His Place in the World. He could handle anything, he thought as he drove up Highway 101 into the hills in search of Cicada Ranch. Even Susan Cade.

By the time he reached the front gate of Cicada Ranch, a white-painted arch supported by stone pillars, he'd shed his tie and loosened his collar. He drove through the open gate, stopped the car and admired the clumps of trees breaking the downward slant of the road and the buff-edged horizon smeared with blue where it misted away into the Pacific. His heart almost singing, Richard took his foot off the brake and drove jauntily onto Cicada Ranch.

The road spilled into a valley about five acres square bounded by tree-crested hills. The house, what Richard could see of it through its screen of acacia trees, was a pleasant Spanish mix of stone and stucco with a red tile roof. The drive curved around the western ell and spread into a macadam before a garage. Split rails supporting yellow roses bordered the drive, and a long stretch of lawn skirted four rectangular barns facing each other across generous paddocks.

Richard parked the Tempo beside the garage, got out and looked around. The ell had latticed windows and a Dutch door, and connected the house to the garage. More rose-grown split rails bounded a service yard. He walked to the open gateway in this fence and read a black-lettered sign beneath a brass bell on the side of the garage—Dr. Susan Cade, D.V.M., and below that—P.H. Cade Racing Stable.

Then he followed a flagstone path to the house and a patio enclosed by a low stone wall. From there, Richard could see a neat stone-and-white-shingle bungalow, hidden from the road by the garage and two massive oaks overhanging its roof. More flagstones hopscotched the lawn to its wide front porch.

It was impressive. No, it was astounding, absolutely goddamned astounding. Meredith and Susan had turned their silly, schoolgirls-in-front-of-the-fire dream into this magnificent place, while he'd been pissing away his trust fund in England.

Richard could see that, too, and no longer felt joyful. He felt deflated and depressed as he backtracked to the bell and gave the rope attached to the clapper a good hard shake. A moment later the screen door giving onto the patio opened. A Spanish woman with creamed-coffee skin, dark braids wound around her head and gold crosses in her pierced ears appeared.

"Good afternoon," he said to her. "I'm Meredith's brother, Richard Parker-Harris."

"Miss Meredith go to look for you," she said, her accent thick, her tone abrupt. "She say you get lost. She say you come I call her on car phone. You wait."

Richard started to ask if Susan was home, or Loren Cade, but the door slapped shut in his face. He glanced at his watch, realized he was an hour and a half later than he'd thought he'd be and shrugged. Oh well. He took off his jacket, tossed it over the back of a redwood chair as a sign that he hadn't gone far and struck off across the grass to explore Cicada Ranch.

The shadows beneath the oaks shading the white bungalow were so deep he didn't see the mostly bald old man sitting on the porch in a rocker until he heard the chair creak. He walked up to the rail and thrust his right hand over it.

"Hello. I'm Richard Parker-Harris, Meredith's brother."

"How do. Rufus Page." The old boy rose slightly to grip Richard's hand, then went back to rocking.

"I'm just having a look around. Lovely place."

Rufus Page grunted and nodded.

"Is Susan around, by any chance? Or her father?"

"Loren be up Solvang way lookin' at some stock. Susie's mos' likely down t'the barns. Meredith took off lookin' fer you some while ago, but I s'pect Consuella told y'that."

"She did, yes. Though I can't imagine why Meredith thought I was lost. She gave me very explicit directions."

"B'lieve she was worried about what you mighta found more'n you gettin' lost."

"I beg your pardon?"

Rufus Page bent his left elbow on the arm of his chair, cocked his wrist and lifted his hand to his mouth, his fingers curved as if holding a glass. Then he winked.

"I see," Richard said tightly. "Thank you."

He turned away with a curt nod and strode toward the barns. He was not a drunk, goddammit. He'd tied one on, you bet, but he'd had good damn reason to. He'd tell Meredith so just as soon as he saw her. And then he'd have a drink. A double, he decided, as he opened the door of the first barn he came to and stepped inside.

A bay and two chestnuts turned their heads toward him, snuffling and flicking their ears. Two whinnies and a deep snort announced his arrival, but no one on two legs appeared. There were only the three horses in the first eighteen stalls. Richard wondered about that and decided they must be mares either ready to foal or about to be bred. This was confirmed when he discovered a right-hand corner at the end of the row, and beyond it three deep wide foaling stalls.

He also found something else that took his breath away—a small, heart-shaped derriere above long, long legs encased in snug, faded denim. The redhead they belonged to was bending sideways over a big-bellied bay mare rubbing a swollen fetlock. Her shiny, deep-auburn hair swept the collar of her shirt, a blue-and-mauve plaid flannel that drew immediate attention to the most magnificent bosom he'd beheld since the last issue of *Playboy*.

Glory, glory did he *love* California. Mesmerized, Richard watched the redhead drop to her heels, set an open bottle of liniment carefully aside in the straw and apply both hands to the puffed-up fetlock.

"Poor Peggity. Poor girl," she crooned in a throaty contralto that sent chills up Richard's back. "I know it hurts, but it'll be over just as soon as you drop this foal."

Dust motes swam in the sunlight streaming through the windows under the eaves, blurred the edges of the long, lazy beams and bathed the stall in buttery warmth. Richard tasted the sharp tang of liniment on his tongue, watched the light gleam on the mare's flanks and tip the redhead's hair with fiery gold. Her fingers were long and lean, her nails short, smooth-looking and clean.

Remarkable in a horse barn. Almost as remarkable as the unexpected well of tenderness Richard felt watching her massage the swollen hoof. He thought of Bea's long, elegant hands guiding his on the piano keys, of Meredith's fingers fumbling the knot out of her white linen stock, tugging it free of her collar and pressing it gently to his broken nose to stanch the flow of blood.

He didn't think of Alfreda or long for the double he'd promised himself once he'd set Meredith straight. He thought of the redhead's fingers soothing away the empty ache inside him, longed for the comfort he somehow knew her touch would bring. Maybe it was jet lag or the warmth of the refracted sunlight on the back of his neck making him light-headed, but Richard didn't think so. The aura of gentleness hovering over the angel in the stall was almost as visible as the straw dust halo shimmering around her glorious hair.

When the bay mare rolled an eye toward him and rumbled, the redhead rose with the liniment bottle in her left hand, the cap in her right, and turned to face Richard. Her nose was straight and perfect, her wide, thickly lashed eyes violet blue, her chin sharp and slightly dimpled.

"Hello." Richard leaned his elbows on the stall door and smiled. "I'm Meredith's brother, Richard. You belong here in some capacity, I hope."

"You could say that." She smiled back at him, her eyes sparkling. "Hello, Richard."

"I'm looking for Dr. Cade. Have you seen her?"

The sparkle went out of her eyes. Richard had the feeling he'd said something wrong, but he couldn't imagine what. With a swift downward glance and a twist of her fingers, she recapped the liniment bottle.

"She's around someplace," she replied, giving the mare an affectionate farewell slap as she started toward him.

She murmured a thank-you when Richard opened the stall door, but kept her gaze averted as she walked into the nearby tack room and placed the liniment bottle on a shelf. Richard had no idea what he'd said to turn her off, but gallantly vowed to put the sparkle back in her eyes.

Until she lifted a fleece-lined denim jacket off a peg inside the door, shrugged into it and his libido got the best of him. What the act of slipping into it did for her bosom he couldn't find words to describe, but he made a mental note to be on hand whenever she next put on a jacket.

"I'm from New York," Richard said, swinging into step beside her as she started past him up the row.

"I know," she replied, quickening her pace.

"Would you like to show me around Santa Barbara? Say later this evening after I buy you dinner?"

She stopped and looked at him askance through her long, dark lashes. "What about Meredith?"

"She won't mind. She hates sight-seeing."

"I know. She always has." She gazed at him steadily, waiting for him, Richard felt, to pick up some clue he'd either dropped or missed completely.

"I'm rushing it, aren't I?" he asked, aching to press himself against her.

"I appreciate the invitation," she said, turning quickly away from him. "But I have to get to the feed store before it closes. Some other time maybe."

"Whatever you say." Richard hurried ahead of her to open the barn door. "How about tomorrow night?"

She started past him but turned abruptly to face him, her shoulder brushing his elbow, her breast his rib cage. She had the most succulent-looking earlobes—unpierced—and the most beautiful voice he'd ever heard. It quavered with indecision and something else Richard couldn't identify as she lifted her eyes briefly to his and said, "I'll think about it."

Then she ducked through the door and walked away from him as fast as she could. Though he wanted to run after her, Richard didn't. Instead he just stepped outside and let the door fall shut behind him. Fleet as a Thoroughbred, she covered the distance between the barns and the car park. He'd never seen anybody in such a tearing hurry to get to a feed store, and frowned, wondering what he'd said to upset her.

Perhaps Susan was still an ogre, perhaps mentioning her had reminded the lush redhead of the forgotten trip to the feed store and Dr. Cade's wrath. Or perhaps—

A jolt of horror shot through Richard. He broke into a run as the redhead all but flung herself behind the wheel of a blue-and-silver Chevy Blazer. He reached the edge of the macadam as the truck squealed out of its parking spot and shot up the road. Out of breath and skidding to a halt, Richard wheeled after it and read the vanity plate on the rear bumper—HOSS-DR.

5

If Meredith hadn't turned wide through the gate, her yellow BMW and Susan's Blazer might have met head-on in the middle of the road. They both hit the brakes, Susan hard enough to fishtail the truck beside the Beemer.

"I told you," she said, leaning her elbow out the window. "I said I had a bad feeling about Richard coming out here. I said the same thing about going to London last spring but you didn't listen. You *never* listen. You're so *sure* you know what's best for everybody, aren't you?"

Susan's eyes glittered. Meredith's stomach clutched.

"What happened?" she asked.

"He asked me out to dinner, that's what happened!"

"But that's *wonderful!* I just *knew* if you two could—"

"Meredith." Susan drew her arm inside the truck and gripped the wheel with both hands. "He had no idea who the hell I am."

Meredith blinked, stunned. "You're kidding."

"I was in the foaling barn with Peggity. He asked me if I'd seen Dr. Cade."

At last Meredith recognized the diamond-bright glitter in her cousin's eyes as unshed tears. "Was he—"

"Sober as a judge," Susan cut in, her jaw clenching.

"I didn't mean *that*. I meant was he wearing his glasses or his contacts?"

"He wasn't wearing his glasses. I didn't ask about his lenses."

"Well maybe—"

"Maybe hell. I'm going to the feed store."

"Susan wait—"

But the truck peeled away, tires squealing. In her side mirror, Meredith watched it shoot through the gate and rocket off down the road. She went to Nieman-Marcus when she was upset; Susan went to the feed store. Damn her anyway. She'd brought Richard out here for *her*.

She'd choke them both, Meredith decided, gritting her teeth as she sped down the hill—Susan once she'd finished feeling sorry for herself over a bin full of oats and Richard just as soon as she parked the car. The idea, she'd tell him, as she shook him until his teeth rattled, was to recognize Susan as the beautiful, intelligent and ga-ga-about-you woman she is, not fail to recognize her *period*.

But Richard wasn't waiting for her when she slammed out of the BMW and stalked toward the house. A Greek god rose from a chair on the patio to meet her, a very angry Greek god, his jaw set, his lustrous blond hair gleaming like quicksilver in the sunset, spreading long shadows across the grass.

My God, he's a hunk. The realization stunned Meredith and stopped her halfway up the flagstone walk. My big brother is a hunk. Turn your back for eight years and something like this happens.

"I could use a drink, Meredith, but I'm not a drunk." Richard shoved his hands on his hips and glowered at her. "What made you think you had to crawl through every bar between here and the airport looking for me?"

His voice was much deeper than she remembered, a wonderfully rich baritone clipped with anger and a faint British accent. It wasn't enough she couldn't decide who he resembled more, Anthony Andrews or Richard Chamberlain, he just *had* to sound like Lawrence Olivier.

"Well I—I mean—yesterday you were—" Meredith stopped herself. She was stammering. She never stammered.

"Of course I was. *Yesterday*," Richard said pointedly. "My fiancée had just dumped me."

"You made a remarkable recovery," Meredith replied, making one of her own. "I understand you asked Susan out to dinner."

"Oh God, don't remind me." Richard forked his right hand through his hair. "You should have been here, Meredith. Or at least warned me. I told you when to expect me. Instead you went haring off and left me to make a perfect ass of myself."

"You were late. I got worried."

"I did a little sight-seeing on the way. I'm not stupid. I can read a map and follow directions."

"I met Susan by the gate. She said you didn't recognize her." Meredith walked up the path onto the patio and stopped in front of him. Up close he was even more dazzling than he was from a distance. "Are you wearing your contacts?"

"Of course I am. I'm blind as a bat without them."

"Then how could you *not* recognize Susan?" Meredith demanded, quelling the urge she felt to slug him. "You've known her half your life!"

"I saw her last at Christmas at Foxglove eight years ago," Richard retorted. "She was thin to the point of being anorexic from the rigors of vet school, and her hair was a god-awful brassy shade of blond—"

"I finally talked her out of bleaching it," Meredith interrupted, "and letting it go natural."

"That's natural?" Richard's eyes widened incredulously. "Then why on earth did she dye it?"

"It's a long story." Meredith sighed and slid her arm through his. "I'll tell you over a cup of tea."

"So long as it's Earl Grey and heavily laced with something that's at least twenty-percent alcohol, I'll listen," Richard replied, lifting his beige tweed jacket from the arm of his chair.

She'd not only let him spike his tea, Meredith decided, as she led him through the mudroom and into the kitchen, she might even join him. Her plan should've worked, dammit. Richard should have recognized Susan, should have taken one look at her and realized she was the woman for him.

What had happened to the dear, dorky Captain-Of-The-Nerd-Team Richard she'd last seen eight years ago? Meredith wondered, watching him drape his jacket over a lattice-back stool at the wood-topped center island. She felt a sudden urge to grab a fistful of his shirt, drag him down to eye-level and say, "Okay, tall, blond and handsome, what'ave you done with my brother?" Instead she filled the teakettle and set it on the stove.

"How was your flight?" she asked, switching on the gas burner as she turned around.

"Bumpy," Richard replied, lifting his pipe and tobacco pouch out of his inside jacket pocket. "Do you mind?"

"Please do." Meredith handed him a yellow ceramic ashtray from the counter. "I want you to feel at home."

An eyebrow several shades darker than his hair arched a fraction, the only hint she'd had so far that wary, distrustful Richard still dwelt within the Chippendale physique. He'd spent his childhood constantly on guard, not that Meredith blamed him, being bounced between Richard Senior, Lady Simpson and Mrs. Barton-Forbes like a beach ball in the stands before an Angels game.

His suspicious, what's-in-it-for-me nature was forgivable once you understood it was a direct result of living in limbo. Where would he be and who would he be this time next week? Tad at Foxglove, Richard with the old harridan in New York, or Dickie, his mother's perfect darling until he misbehaved or she grew bored with parenthood and decided to go skiing in Saint Moritz.

"Well thank you, Meredith." The eyebrow lowered and Richard slid onto the stool. "I'll do my best."

He always did, which was the reason Meredith had hated his guts when they were children. Until Susan had explained he couldn't help himself, that he drove himself to be perfect so he wouldn't be sent away again. But he always was.

He was so unhappy, she'd said, he felt so unloved and unwanted. And then she'd burst into tears. Meredith had never seen her tough-as-horseshoe-nails cousin cry before. It had frightened her so badly she'd run for her mother.

"You seem to be doing very nicely." Richard opened his leather tobacco pouch and began filling his pipe. "Lovely home, gorgeous spread. Apparently dreams do come true."

"Sure they do." Meredith pulled the shrieking teakettle off the burner. "If you work at them hard enough."

She poured boiling water over two bags in a china pot, put on the lid and a cozy knitted by Consuella, then turned around to watch Richard light his pipe. She noted the strong line of his jaw as he drew the flame, his long, supple fingers. The signet ring Richard Senior had given him on his twenty-first birthday was on his left hand. Meredith had last seen it, fleetingly and through binoculars, on a chain around Lady Alfreda's throat. So had Susan.

"Glad you got your ring back," she said, lifting the teapot and the sugar bowl, mugs and the creamer onto the island. "She looked the type to keep it."

Richard nearly bit through the stem of his pipe. Meredith would have gladly bitten her tongue, but it was too late; she'd already spilled the beans.

"How do you know about my ring?" he asked, his eyebrow sliding up again.

"Luke and Susan and I were at Epsom last spring for the English Derby." Meredith hiked herself onto the stool opposite Richard and filled the mugs. "I saw Lady Alfreda in the paddock before the race. I also saw your ring around her neck on that dopey chain and wanted to strangle her with it."

That was a lie. Susan had wanted to strangle her with it. Until she'd taken a good long look at Lady Alfreda through binoculars. Then she'd spun shakily on Meredith.

"Why do I listen to you?" she'd demanded. "Why do I let you talk me into things like this? I can't compete with her!"

Then she'd run off the racecourse with Meredith behind her trying to talk her into staying. They hadn't seen Richard and hadn't expected to—not in the paddock anyway—and they'd missed the Derby. No wonder Susan had gone to the feed store.

"I was glad Alfreda's horse finished last," Meredith said peevishly.

Richard sighed and reached for the cream. "I lost a bundle on that nag."

"Luke made out like a bandit. His winnings nearly paid for our trip."

"And Susan? How did she do on the tote?"

"Susan doesn't bet on horses anymore."

"Really?" Richard poured cream down the side of his mug, hastily put the pitcher aside and wiped the spill with a napkin. "When did she give it up?"

"Once we'd made enough to buy Cicada and Flagmaster and put Uncle Loren through the Betty Ford Clinic so the P. H. Cade Racing Stable would have the best trainer in the world."

"Tell me you're joking, Meredith." Richard gave her a hard look. "Don't tell me that old monster Flagmaster is here. And if he is, tell me he's stuffed like Trigger."

"He's alive and well in his own private barn and reinforced paddock. He's also sired an incredible string of colts. Here. Read this." Meredith snatched a flyer off the stack on the counter behind her and gave it to Richard. "We're pitting Banner, the best of Flagmaster's get so far, against Roundhouse Stables' Derby hopeful, High Brow. It's for charity, of course, and—"

"Meredith." Richard slapped the flyer down, unread, on the island. "Flagmaster was disqualified from the Belmont for biting the starter. It took six grooms and damn near a tranquilizer gun to get him off the track."

"True," Meredith granted, "but he broke Secretariat's Derby and Preakness records."

"He'll break your silly neck, too, if he gets half a chance. Even Dad said he was crazy, dangerously crazy, and there are very few horses the old man can't handle."

"There isn't a horse that's ever been foaled that Susan can't handle," Meredith declared proudly. "Flagmaster eats out of her hand."

"Kindred spirits." Richard picked up the flyer, gave it a cursory read, then glanced at Meredith. "Susan *never* bets on the horses?"

"Never," Meredith replied, stirring sugar into her tea. "Since she can read their minds she thinks it's taking unfair advantage. She always did, if you'll recall."

"Yes, I remember that now." Richard laid the flyer aside, picked up his mug but didn't drink, just sat staring at it pensively.

Meredith remembered Susan saying there was more than Lady Alfreda bothering him. She opened her mouth to ask what it was, but shut it as Loren Cade stepped through the door from the mudroom into the kitchen.

His boots were filthy and muck-caked. There was a shoe scraper and a boot rack just outside the door, but no amount of begging from Susan or screaming in Spanish from Consuella could persuade Loren Cade to use them. He'd simply grin the boyish cowboy grin he aimed at Richard as he offered his hand and say his feet got cold without his boots.

"Nice t'see you again, Richard. Pleased you could come out for Meredith's weddin'."

"I wouldn't miss it, Loren." Richard rose and shook his hand. "Good to see you, too."

Meredith watched her uncle watch Richard. If Loren felt any surprise at the transformation he'd undergone in the eight years since they'd all last seen Richard, he managed to hide it.

"How'd you make out in Solvang?" she asked.

"Didn't see no mares worth buyin' and puttin' to Flagmaster," Loren replied, ambling toward the refrigerator. "Sure do wish you could sweet-talk that High Brow filly outta Luke. Found a nice little bloodline she would."

"I'm working on him, Uncle Loren." Meredith leaned her elbow on the island, her chin on her fist, and watched her uncle take two pieces of bread out of a loaf, squirt them with mustard, slap a slice of ham between them and shut the fridge, leaving a dollop of mustard dripping down the side of the plastic squeeze bottle and the bread wrapper open.

"Where's Susie?" Loren asked, filling a mug from the coffeemaker on the counter and stirring sugar into it with the handle of the knife he'd used to spread mustard.

"At the feed store," Meredith said.

"That so." Loren's gaze slid first toward Richard and then Meredith over the rim of his cup as he drank. "S'pect I oughta wash up 'fore she gits back or Consuella comes in to start supper an' catches me trackin' up her clean floor."

"I s'pect you better," Meredith agreed.

Loren chewed and swallowed the last of his sandwich and gave Richard a clap on the shoulder that nearly knocked him off his stool. "We'll have us a nice long jaw after supper, son," he said, and strolled out the door.

6

DURING SUPPER Susan said very little and didn't look at Richard. Not once, even though he sat across from her at the oak trestle table in the dining room. He tried to pay attention to Loren Cade, who was telling him about his trip to Solvang, but found himself distracted by the candlelight shimmering on Susan's hair.

He couldn't figure out how the ugly duckling he remembered had become a swan, though he was pretty sure it went deeper than peroxide and blond toner. He did his best to be charming and put the sparkle back in Susan's eyes, but she remained aloof. And her gaze remained averted.

When she excused herself before dessert and headed for her office, Richard's mouth went dry as he watched her slip past the Spanish grille separating the dining room from the living room and start down the stone-floored hallway. Her figure was the stuff of erotic dreams, lush and willow-slim in cream wool slacks and a teal cowl-neck sweater.

Desire flashed through him hot and quick. He would've gladly given his slab of gooseberry pie, his favorite, to follow Susan. If Meredith hadn't gone all out with candles and her grandmother's china he would have—and the cool, appraising glint in Loren Cade's blue eyes be damned.

"Bring your pipe, son," Loren said, rising with his coffee cup in hand. "We'll have us a smoke and a catch-up."

Richard followed Loren Cade, retrieved his pipe from the island in the kitchen on the way, and joined him in front of the fire hissing and snapping in the stone hearth in the great room.

Susan's father hadn't changed much since Richard had last seen him at Foxglove. There was a bit more gray in his reddish-brown hair, and a healthy tan in lieu of his once dissipated pallor. He waved Richard into one of two upholstered armchairs in front of the fireplace, put his cup on a small table, and lit a cigarette from a crumpled pack in his shirt pocket.

The smoke flared Richard's nostrils and made his mouth water. He hadn't yearned for a cigarette in years, not since he'd given them up for his pipe, which he laid aside in favor of savoring Loren's secondhand smoke.

"Hear tell you're engaged t'be married," Loren said, exhaling through his nose.

"I was," Richard replied, "until my fiancée gave my ring back four days ago."

"Well." Loren pronounced it "whale," drew deep on his cigarette and exhaled. "Sorry t'hear it."

"Don't be. I'm not. It was a dreadful mistake."

"Why's that?"

"I don't love Alfreda." Richard shifted in his chair, surprised at the twinge he felt in his shoulder where Loren had clapped him one, a good one, on his way out of the kitchen. "I never did. I realize that now."

"'Parently, she didn't love you, neither."

Richard smiled ruefully. "Apparently."

"Whale." Loren leaned back and bent his elbow on the arm of his chair. A thin trail of smoke from the cigarette pinched between his fingers drifted toward the fire. "Reckon she done you a favor."

"Now that you mention it, I suppose she did."

"Fascinatin' creatures, women. Can't never tell what they're thinkin'. Know why?" Loren leaned forward and gave Richard a sage, narrowed-eye nod through a haze of smoke. "'Cause they don't. They just feel. They ain't ashamed of it. And they ain't afraid of it, neither. Not like us men. Woman's kinda like a horse that way—"

He pronounced it "hoss" rendering Richard temporarily deaf in a shameful rush of memory. Elocution lessons had quickly rid Susan of her nasal native twang, but Loren still sounded like a bad Hank Williams imitation. The first Christmas he'd come to Foxglove, it had been Richard Senior's turn to host the annual holiday hunt breakfast. Loren had gone around the room, pleasantly half-lit, telling one and all he was Loren Cade, Susie's father, from "Oplahoma."

The next day, Richard dragged out the *Rand McNally Road Atlas* and asked Susan to point out Oplahoma. When spring came and he was forced to join the Junior Hunt Club trail ride, he'd amused one and all by singing Rogers and Hammerstein's "Oklahoma," popping his index finger in his cheek to make it "Oh-oh-oh-oh-*OP*-lahoma." Susan had ridden ahead of him, ramrod straight in her saddle, the back of her neck splotched with red.

What a rotten, mean little shit, Richard thought, remembering all too well the skinny little snob he'd been in Saville Row tweeds and polished leather boots. He'd pushed Susan's buttons, all right, and he'd done it again when he'd asked her if she'd seen Dr. Cade. At this rate, he'd never get her to the track, he thought, dragging his attention back to Loren.

"If a hoss don't love t'run," he was saying, "there ain't no whip with sting enough and no jockey smart enough gonna make 'im. But if a hoss runs just for the sheer joy of runnin', he'll run till his heart bursts. Same with a woman, son. Same with a woman."

"Absolutely, Loren. I couldn't agree more. Would you excuse me?" Richard rose from his chair and backtracked to the dining room, where Rufus Page was still wolfing gooseberry pie and Consuella was helping Meredith clear the table around him. "How does Susan take her coffee?"

"Black with one sugar," Meredith replied, watching him fill two cups from the china server on the sideboard.

"Will I be disturbing her?"

Meredith smiled. "I'm sure of it."

"Good." Richard set his jaw and started down the hall balancing two steaming cups on wafer-thin saucers. High damn time he disturbed her. He'd kill for a cigarette, had almost bummed one from Loren, yet craved more than nicotine. He yearned for something he couldn't put a name to, something he suspected lay at the end of the hall with Susan Cade.

It was crazy, lunatic, yet the longing he felt made the balloon in his chest swell and ache as he stopped in her open office doorway and saw her sitting behind her desk, the old mahogany one that used to reside in the library at Foxglove until Richard had carved his initials into it. Bea hadn't said a word. She'd simply moved the blotter to hide the scratches and told his father she was changing the room's decor.

Richard had forgotten the incident and the need he'd felt to put his mark on something as proof that he belonged until now. Until Susan lifted her head with a start and looked at him. It took Richard a second to pull himself out of the memory, to loosen his grip on the hot sticky handle of his penknife and smile at her.

"I brought your coffee," he said, starting into the room. "Black with one sugar."

"Thank you." She straightened in her ladder-back wooden chair—to put as much distance as possible between them, Richard was certain. He placed the cup and saucer in front of her and sat in the chair before the desk. It matched Susan's and was every bit as hard and unforgiving as her stare.

"I'm sorry I didn't recognize you." Richard put his cup on the desk, laid his elbows on the arms of his chair and laced his fingers together. "I wasn't expecting you. I was expecting the Susan Cade I remembered."

Her unyielding gaze didn't so much as flicker, though the fire burning across the room did. The flames didn't reach far enough to soften the harsh glare of the green-shaded banker's lamp on the desk corner that showed weary shadows under Susan's eyes and the corner of the boyishly awkward "R" peeking out from under the corner of a dog-eared manila folder.

"The troglodyte, you mean. The one with braces, terminal acne and bleached hair."

"I always wondered why it looked like moldy straw."

She smiled. Just barely. "That's probably the nicest thing anybody ever said about my hair."

"I can't imagine why you changed the color."

"Teenage girls do stupid things." Susan shrugged. "At the time I wanted to look like Meredith."

"For God's sake, why?" Richard asked, genuinely amazed.

"I thought if I looked like her I'd be able to act like her. I figured I'd fit in, then, and everyone would love me."

Susan shut the folder, revealing an arrow-pierced heart someone—probably one of Meredith's dopey little preppy friends who used to trail behind him, dreamy-eyed—had drawn around his initials. Unlike the crude RP-H Richard had gouged into the rock-hard mahogany, whoever had drawn Cupid's trademark had done so with great care and near perfection.

"I also thought if I looked like Meredith," Susan went on, sliding the folder over the scratches, "I wouldn't have to be scared all the time that I'd be sent away."

She raised her eyes to his face. In the fireplace a log broke with a plop, momentarily sending the flames high enough to gleam in her eyes and lick a provocative shadow along the curve of her jaw.

The nape of Richard's neck prickled. He had a feeling Susan had said something important, but for the life of him he couldn't figure out what.

"I'd really like to take you to dinner," he said.

"I've no intention of holding you to that, Richard."

"But I have every intention of holding *you* to it," he said. Just as close, just as tight and just as soon as I can, he thought.

"I wish I could tell when you're being sincere and not just polite." Susan lifted her hand to her forehead and spread her fingers on her temple. Richard wondered if it was a nervous gesture or if she had a headache. "You said thank-you when I helped you up after I broke your nose. For years I thought you meant thank-you for breaking your nose."

"Thank you, Susan, for helping me up."

"You're welcome." She smiled. "I'm sorry I broke your nose."

"Apology accepted. Where shall we have dinner?"

"I'll go on one condition. Tell me *honestly* why you asked me."

"I would, but then you wouldn't go."

"Try me."

"Just so I could look at you. Preferably across a table lit with candles."

Susan's eyes began to sparkle. "I was hoping you'd say that."

7

RICHARD SPENT the next day sight-seeing, changing his British pounds for dollars, and buying white underwear. The salesclerk at Nordstrom's gave him a strange look when he requested the use of a dressing room, but led him into one. He threw away the last pair of briefs Alfreda had bought him—patterned with the British Union Jack—and left the store feeling a bit more like himself.

It was the first hint at a genuine, solid identity he'd had in a long time. Now all he had to do was figure out how (he knew damn good and well why) he'd developed an insane desire to go to bed with a woman he'd spent half his life despising.

If only he could mesh memory with reality, meld the filthy ragamuffin Loren Cade had sent to Foxglove with the glorious creature Susan had become. If he could just get a grip on the gut-wrenching seesaw between his head and his heart, between loathing and lust. . . .

But he couldn't, not even with the pack of cigarettes he bought and chain-smoked. Focus on getting Susan to the track, he told himself, not into bed. But that's all he could think about as he strolled the balmy streets and boulevards of Santa Barbara.

In the window of a saddlery shop he discovered a poster blown up from the flyer Meredith had shown him, advertising the charity match race between High Brow, the Kentucky Derby hopeful from Roundhouse Stables, and Banner, the best of the P. H. Cade Racing Stable. A sun-faded article from the society page was taped next to the poster, and Richard forgot his dilemma for the hour or so he spent looking it up in the periodicals section of the library.

The washed-out picture of Meredith, a founding patroness of Rainbow's End, an organization devoted to fulfilling the dreams of disadvantaged children, made Richard smile. And wonder why Susan, though she was quoted in the piece, had chosen not to be photographed.

Richard also learned from the article that Meredith was a highly successful investment counselor with a string of millionaire clients. While he'd been blowing his inheritance on Alfreda, Meredith had earned an MBA from Stanford and parlayed her own trust fund into a sizable fortune.

It was another swift kick in the ego, another reminder that he'd pissed his life away with his money, but it was something else to think about besides the dark voice speaking from the depths of his psyche. *A leopard can't change its spots. The bully who broke your nose and humiliated you in front of your father is still lurking somewhere inside that fall-on-your-knees-and-drool gorgeous body.*

A leopard can't change its spots. It was a cliché, but a sobering one. As sobering as remembering that Susan's arrival at Foxglove had virtually destroyed Richard's already-precarious relationship with his father. She'd rapidly become the daredevil, horse-loving son Richard Senior had despaired of ever having. Bea had thrown herself body and soul into the challenge of making a lady out of her, and Richard had been forgotten. He'd never forgiven Susan for it, or himself for so desperately needing a place to belong.

When he phoned Cicada Ranch at five he almost hoped Susan wouldn't be there, but she was. She gave him the address of the restaurant where they were to meet and said she'd be there by seven.

At six-thirty Richard found a florist and bought Susan a single yellow rose wrapped in green tissue paper. He carried it back to the rented Tempo and laid it gently on the seat while he peeled off his sweater, put on the jacket he'd hung on a hanger in the back seat and got in behind the wheel to knot his tie in the rearview mirror.

Then he turned the ignition key—and swore when the engine didn't start. He got out and opened the hood, fiddled with the spark plugs and the distributor cap, tried twice more to start the car and gave up at ten minutes before seven.

He raced for the nearest pay phone, fumbled through the Yellow Pages, found the number of the restaurant and slid a quarter into the coin slot. He left a message for Dr. Cade, then called the rental company. The tow truck they sent showed up at 7:55. The driver jump-started the dead battery and gave Richard directions to the restaurant.

He arrived at twenty minutes past eight, ducked into the men's room to wash the grease off his hands and presented himself to the maître d', who told him Dr. Cade had left some time ago. He also claimed to know nothing about a phone message left for her. Richard sprinted, cursing, back to the Tempo and drove like a maniac for Cicada Ranch.

When he burst through the kitchen door, panting, winded and with his hair falling over his eyes, Susan was standing at the island sipping a cup of coffee and flipping through the evening paper. She wore an emerald-green silk dress with a flowing skirt, a plunging neckline and a bolero jacket.

God, she was beautiful.

And mad as hell. He saw it in the sparkle in her eyes as she glanced at him over her shoulder, slammed her cup down, and started around the island with coffee splatters on the front of her dress. She made for the door in stiff, angry strides and two-inch heels dyed to match her dress. She had ankles like a Thoroughbred. Richard imagined he could span them with his thumb and index finger, and have room to spare.

"Susan, please wait."

"Did you get lost?" She spun around on the opposite side of the island. "Or did you just chicken out?"

"The goddamn battery in the rental car died."

"Oh really? Then how did you get here?"

"I called the rental company. They sent a tow truck."

"Why didn't you call me?"

"I did. I left a message for you at the restaurant."

"I never got it. I waited an hour." Susan snatched a napkin out of a wicker basket on the island and scrubbed angrily at the coffee spots on her dress.

The silk was probably ruined. So was any chance Richard had of getting her within ten miles of a betting window. He couldn't believe Susan didn't believe him. He was furious with her for thinking any man in his right mind would stand her up. But mostly he was furious with himself for thinking first and foremost that if she stayed mad he'd never get her to the track, let alone into bed.

He wanted both, God help him. More than he'd ever wanted anything in his life. More than he'd ever thought he wanted Alfreda or his father's approval he wanted Susan. So suddenly and so overwhelmingly that he nearly took her right there on the kitchen floor and the consequences be damned. Instead he carried the yellow rose to the island and laid it in front of her.

The napkin went still in her hand. Susan blinked, touched the grease-smudged tissue paper, then glanced up at Richard. Her eyes still sparkled, but there was enough uncertainty in them to give him hope.

"I wouldn't have brought you your favorite color rose if I hadn't intended to show up," he said, and felt Susan's visible jolt of surprise in an electric shiver up the back of his neck.

"Yellow roses are *not* my favorite."

"Yes, they are."

The certainty Richard felt amazed him. And frightened Susan. He didn't know why, but he saw it in her eyes, in the dilation of her pupils and the tremble of her chin.

"Meredith doesn't know everything about me," Susan retorted. "She just *thinks* she does."

"I didn't ask her. I just knew yellow was your favorite."

Richard had no idea how he knew, and couldn't have cared less. He edged closer to the island and Susan, and laid his hand gently over hers. She snatched it away, took a step backward and rubbed her hand against her skirt as if it burned.

"Just this once I wish you'd been polite," she said, and spun away from him on her heel.

8

SUSAN FLED as far as the fireplace in the living room, snatched up the poker and stirred the charred bits in the hearth to make sure the fire had gone out. She tried to make herself feel as dead as the ashes but couldn't. It was impossible with her awareness of Richard's aching and yearning and the panic swirling through her mind.

He didn't know yellow roses are my favorite. It was just a lucky guess. They grow all over this place, for heaven's sake. He couldn't possibly *know* unless . . . But that was impossible. Meredith told him. Please God she told him.

Susan put the poker back and looked at her hands. They were steady. Cold and clammy but steady, even though she could still feel Richard's fingers squeezing hers. Her insides quaked from the intensity of the emotions swirling through her—her own as well as Richard's—but it didn't show.

Not that Richard would care if it did, Susan thought bitterly, walking to the Christmas tree Meredith had knocked herself silly to put up before his arrival and knelt to unplug the lights. She'd loved Richard so long that she could hardly draw a breath knowing all he did was want her.

Biting back tears, Susan reached for the plug, her breath catching as she saw Richard's reflection, stretched and warped out of shape on the curve of a blue spun-glass ornament. She turned her head to look at him, her heart constricting in her chest. His collar was unbuttoned, his

tie askew, his hands loose at his sides. The kitchen light
shining behind him gave him a halo and blurred his fea-
tures. Susan was glad she couldn't see his face.

"Was there something else?" she asked coolly.

"Yes, there is."

He came swiftly across the room, dropped to his knees
in front of her, grabbed her shoulders, pulled her against
him, and kissed her hard on the mouth. He didn't force her
lips apart and he didn't hurt her. He just kept his mouth
locked against hers until she could feel her teeth. Then he
held her at arm's length and looked at her, his jaw tight.

"That's all I've wanted to do since I saw you in the barn
yesterday, but that's not *all* I want to do. Shall I tell you
the rest or should I show you?"

Even without her gift, Susan would have known what
he wanted. She heard it in the tremor in his voice, felt it in
the heat building between them at hip and breast where
their bodies touched.

There was no point telling Richard she knew how he felt.
He wouldn't believe her. Anymore than he'd believe her if
she told him he was the only dream she'd ever had that
hadn't come true. She'd dreamed of being a vet and she
was one, a damn good one. Her father was sober and had
been for five years. She owned her own place and her own
horses.

Susan had never settled for second best in her life, but
maybe—just this once—half a dream was better than
none. It was a rationalization and she knew it. Just like she
knew this might be her only chance to find out what it felt
like to be in Richard's arms.

"Show me," she said, slipping her hands inside his
jacket.

The movement brought them tightly together. Susan
felt the heat of his arousal, the tension in his muscles as she

spread her palms on his back, saw the flare of his nostrils as she lifted her chin to look at him. The tree lights flickered in his eyes and on his cheekbones as he bent his mouth toward hers.

Susan parted her lips, but he didn't kiss her, just softly drew his nose up the length of hers to trace the arch of her brow. Gooseflesh shot up her back, as much from the jolt of surprise she felt as the brush of his nose across the delicate skin of her forehead.

Susan *knew* he'd meant to kiss her but hadn't. How had he done that? It confused her, frightened her like the rose had, but thrilled her and made her whimper as his mouth came to rest on the pulse beating in her temple. She closed her eyes and felt it beneath his lips, heard the noise he made in his throat, felt it vibrate in her head and prickle up her spine in a second rush of gooseflesh that left her trembling and shaken.

"Oh Susan." Richard whispered raggedly, his voice raw as he dragged his lips along the curve of her jaw.

Oh Susan what? She groped for the rest of the thought, stretched her senses toward his as she sometimes had to do with Flagmaster when he was being difficult, but there was nothing coherent to lock on to. Only the swirl of Richard's emotions, vibrantly incandescent colors shooting like tracer bullets through his mind.

"Oh *say it*, please," Susan said, unaware that she'd spoken until she heard her own unsteady voice.

"Say what?" Richard murmured, his lips moving provocatively near the corner of her mouth.

A chill laced across the nape of Susan's neck as he slipped his hands beneath her arms and gently circled her waist. *Say you love me*, she begged silently, even though she knew he didn't. *Please say you love me.*

"Say anything," she said, then gasped as his hands slid up her rib cage and curved beneath her breasts.

"You're so beautiful. So very beautiful."

The rough-edged growl in his voice shot a thrill through Susan. Half a dream wasn't so bad after all. A smile tugging one corner of her mouth, she brushed her nose against Richard's, then drew away and opened her eyes.

He was looking at her, but not at her face. He was staring at her breasts cupped in his hands, his lips parted, his eyes heavy-lidded. He was having trouble breathing, but so was Susan. She felt like she'd been kicked in the heart, but before she could push him away, he brushed her nipples with his thumbs, lightly, so softly she could barely feel it. Susan ached to feel more, swayed against him, reaching—then sucked in a breath and held it when he touched her again, drew circles with his thumbs and she *knew* what touching her felt like to Richard.

It was only a flash, lasted only a fraction of a heartbeat, but it was enough to dissolve the thought of pushing him away. She yielded to him.

Sliding his right arm around her to cushion the back of her neck, Richard eased her to the floor and stretched himself beside her. His left hand still cupped her breast, his thumb drawing circles until he lowered his head and took her nipple, lush green silk and all, into his mouth.

Colors exploded in Susan's head, shooting like hot-tailed comets through her senses. *Oh love me, Richard. Just a little.* She murmured it over and over in her mind, tried to reach again to touch him. *Love me, Richard, please love me.*

"I *am*, Susan," he said, raising his head to look at her.

"What?" She blinked at him.

"You said," Richard replied with a soft, smoky-voiced smile, "love me."

"But I—" *Didn't say it aloud,* she finished inside her head. Or did I, Susan wondered, catching her bottom lip between her teeth.

"But what?" Richard prodded gently.

I must have said it aloud, Susan decided. I must have.

"Never mind," she replied, twining her arms around his neck. "Just kiss me."

He did, hungrily, but still not forcing her lips apart. *Love me, Richard.* Susan quivered as his hand slid down to caress her hip and lift her skirt. *Love me, love me.* She raised her knee, felt the silken hem of her dress slide up her leg, and shivered as Richard's fingertips followed it.

"Oh God." He dragged his mouth away from hers, buried his lips in the curve of her throat and clasped her thigh. "Oh Susan."

"Oh Susan what?" She murmured, raising one hand to stroke his hair.

"Oh Susan I—"

Over the pounding of her heart—or was it Richard's—Susan heard the rattle of the loose knob on the door between the kitchen and the mudroom. "'Lo, Susie," her father called. "You still up?"

She was in a flash, and so was Richard. He yanked her skirt over her knees, she smudged a smear of lipstick from the corner of his mouth. Richard raked his fingers through his hair. Susan smoothed her chin-length bob.

"Yo, Susie?" Loren Cade called again, the ring of his boot heels on the stone floor drawing closer.

"In here!" Susan called, cringing at the warble in her voice and throwing Richard a panicky look.

He touched her chin with his fingertips, then leaned nonchalantly on the heel of his left hand and raised his right knee to prop his elbow. Susan glanced toward the kitchen, saw her father backlit in the archway, then nothing but a dazzle as he hit the wall switch that turned on the living-room lamps. Turning her head away, she blinked madly to clear her vision.

"Evening, Loren," Richard said smoothly.

Was his voice really four octaves deeper than usual or did it just sound that way over the mad thud of her pulse in her ears? Susan held her breath and waited for her father to answer.

"Evenin', Richard," he replied, his Oklahoma drawl just a tad slower than usual.

Forcing her eyes to stay open, Susan turned her head and smiled at her father. "Want some coffee? We were just having some."

Loren looked down his hooked, one-quarter Cherokee nose at her. "That why your cup's out here in the kitchen?"

"So *that's* where I left it." Susan snapped her fingers. "Silly me, crawling around on the floor looking for it under the tree."

"'Specially with the lights out," Loren said flatly. "I'll just pour me a cup."

He turned out of the doorway, his boot heels ringing on the hard floor. Susan hid her face against Richard's shoulder.

"He didn't buy it," she whispered.

"Of course he didn't."

"What a stupid thing to say. I'm sorry, Richard."

"Don't be, Susan. We are adults." He raised her chin on his index finger. "I'm only sorry I didn't take you to my room. I wish now that I had."

"Be careful what you wish for," Susan warned softly. "You just might get it."

9

That's what Richard was afraid of, knowing Susan wanted him as much as he wanted her. And that he would, God help him, take her the next chance he got. Preferably after he took her to the track, but he wouldn't let that stop him. It kept him awake half the night in the Navajo-motif guest room. In his brand-new white underwear, with the same old doubts gnawing at him, knees drawn up, bare heels braced on the bed frame, he smoked one of the last of his cigarettes down to the filter.

The second thing that scared him was knowing he'd move heaven and hell to get her alone and out of her clothes at the earliest possible moment; the third was knowing what a son of a bitch he was for even thinking about doing the things he wanted to do to Susan unless he loved her. Which he didn't.

Which Susan knew as well as he did. Still, it took all her self-control once they'd said good-night under Loren's watchful eye, not to slip down the hall into the guest room two doors away, out of her pink pajamas and into his bed.

More than she'd ever wanted anything Susan wanted Richard, but from experience she knew you could want something too much. As badly as she'd wanted to be an equine vet, the course work and internship had nearly killed her. The only thing that kept her in her room was knowing that as much as she loved Richard it probably would kill her when he walked out of her life—more than likely two minutes after Meredith and Luke said "I do."

While Richard smoked himself into a headache, Susan paced her mostly white-and-brass bedroom until her back ached, wishing she could take back what she'd said to him. She fell asleep only minutes after he did, spread-eagled on the bed, and woke with a start only slightly ahead of him, a little after nine. She awoke from a lushly erotic dream, tangled in eyelet sheets and a white silk comforter, and an hour late for rounds at Roundhouse.

Susan occasionally overslept; Dr. Susan Cade, never. Sweeping her hair out of her eyes, she fumbled for the bedside phone and called Luke. Once he'd razzed the hell out of her, he told her not to rush.

So she didn't, just took a moody soak in the oversize tub in her bathroom. While she sank up to her chin in indecision and lavender-scented bubbles, Richard braced his hands on the ceramic tile wall of the guest bath shower, jaw set, teeth grinding, unsated erection throbbing in the hot, steamy spray. Susan shaved her legs while he shaved his face. She dressed for work in jeans, a red-and-black flannel houndstooth shirt over a black turtleneck and her trusty Dingo boots. Richard tugged an ecru cotton knit sweater over his head, stuck toilet paper on his chin and smoked his last cigarette.

While Susan used the curling iron on the ends of her hair, she swore not to be weak. Or stupid. She was woman. She was strong. Richard simply swore, gritting his teeth as he gingerly zipped himself into a pair of tan corduroys.

Susan made her bed, resolving not to make a fool of herself over a man who would use her and leave her. She'd gotten over Richard before; she'd get over him again. Richard resolved to give up cigarettes and searched the ashtray for a butt worth smoking.

When the scream came, they both bolted for the kitchen. Susan hit the hallway as the guest room doorway opened and Richard came through it. They stopped and stared at each other.

Richard felt a pang at the tired smudges under Susan's eyes, wanted to press her cheek to his shoulder and rock her to sleep. Susan wanted to kiss the nick on his chin.

"Who screamed?" he asked.

"Consuella, probably," Susan replied. "She usually does when Dad comes in with stable muck all over his boots."

Richard had no idea who moved first. Neither did Susan. One moment they were standing looking at each other, the next moment his arms were around her and his mouth was clamped over hers in a fierce kiss. Susan tasted like toothpaste and salvation; Richard like tobacco and need.

The tobacco was new, the need wasn't. It had always been there, so deep and so painful it hurt just to brush against. What frightened Susan into pushing him away was the realization that it was the need of a man now. Not a boy who'd wait to be invited, but a man capable of taking what she hadn't yet decided to give.

"This is wrong," she said, holding him at arm's length. "We don't like each other. We don't know each other. Not anymore. Not well enough for this."

"I think we've known each other plenty long enough for this," Richard replied. "And I think it's what's been wrong between us from the jump."

The same thing had occurred to Susan a long time ago. It was one of her favorite Richard Fantasies. She had a million of them. In this one he suddenly came to his senses on the eve of his wedding to Lady Alfreda What's-Her-Title, and hopped the first Concorde bound for California to declare his just-realized but undying love for her—

a variation of the old-knight-in-shining-armor-sweeping-to-the-rescue-on-a-white-charger theme. Except there wasn't a white charger within four hundred years of Cicada Ranch, and the only place Richard wanted to sweep her was off to bed.

"I was twelve," Susan retorted, folding her arms defensively. "I couldn't even spell sex."

"I was almost fifteen. I could spell it in six languages."

"I was a troglodyte. You said so yourself."

"When hormones rule your life, looks don't matter."

He didn't mean it the way it sounded, but that's how Susan took it. Richard saw it in the flinch of her shoulders, the upward jerk of her chin a second before she spun away from him and stalked toward the kitchen.

"Susan wait," he said, rushing after her. He reached for her elbow, but she shrugged him off. Quickening his pace, he lowered his voice as they neared the kitchen doorway and he tried again to catch her.

"What I meant was—" Richard forgot what he meant as they cleared the archway and he came to a startled halt a step behind Susan.

Meredith stood at the island slicing a frothy white pile of tulle to ribbons with a pocket knife. Not a sissy knife like he'd used on the mahogany desk, but a workingman's knife with a serious blade. Since Loren Cade sat calmly on a stool beside her, watching as he smoked a cigarette, Richard figured the knife was his. He also figured Meredith was the one who'd screamed, and guessed that it had something to do with whatever it was she was viciously slicing to bits.

"Meredith, is that your wedding veil?" Susan asked. "The one you've been waiting six weeks to be delivered?"

"Eight," Meredith snapped, the knife ripping audibly through another layer of tulle.

Little puffs of it caught in her hair; one floated into Loren Cade's coffee mug. He fished it out with his finger, picked up the mug and took a healthy swallow.

"Then why," Susan asked, "are you cutting it to shreds?"

"Because my dress is ivory, Susan. *Ivory.* This veil is *white.*" Meredith slammed the knife down on the island and glared at her. "Pure as the driven snow, untouched, virginal *white.* Just like you."

This time Susan didn't flinch, she recoiled. Richard stood close enough to feel it, close enough to hear the breath she sucked in and watch the color drain from her face. It came back almost instantly in a vivid flush, as she squared her shoulders and made quickly for the back door.

"Susan, I'm sorry," Meredith apologized, whirling after her. "I didn't meant that. You know I—"

"I'm late for rounds." Susan's voice and the ring of her boot heels on the stone floor echoed behind her as she crossed the mudroom. "Have a nice day making confetti."

And making Susan an object of pity, if what Meredith said was true. The possibility made Richard's stomach clench. Once upon a time, he would have loved tormenting Susan with something like this, which is what she was probably thinking. Only she was wrong.

The inside back door slammed behind her, hard enough to rattle the glass and lift Loren Cade's head from his coffee mug. From the corner of one eye, Richard saw him swivel his stool toward him, and Meredith spin after him as he started purposefully after Susan.

"Where are you going, Richard?"

"To stop her," he said, all but running out of the house.

But he had to catch her first and that didn't seem likely. She'd already reached the foot of the flagstone path. Richard vaulted the patio wall, intending to take a shortcut across the lawn. Instead he skidded to a halt on the dew-wet grass when he saw Susan drag a sleeve across her eyes.

Meredith and me and our big mouths, he thought, watching her fling open the door of the Blazer and leap behind the wheel. Listening to the gun of the engine and the squeal of the tires as Susan backed the truck in a hard half circle, he wished he could erase the past forty-eight hours. Not to mention the past fifteen years.

But he couldn't, no matter how badly he wanted to, so he just stood watching the bright morning sun flash on the hood of the Blazer as it shot up the road toward the gate. When the screen door creaked behind him, he glanced over his shoulder at Meredith, standing on the patio chewing her lip.

"Was Susan crying?" she asked.

"I think so." Richard walked back to her, eyed her soberly and asked, "So is she or isn't she?"

"Is she or isn't she what?"

"Don't play games with me. Is Susan or isn't she—"

A scream twice as bloodcurdling as Meredith's cut him off and spun her around on one foot. "Oh God—Consuella," she said, bolting for the door just as Loren Cade came scooting through it with a battered straw Stetson in one hand.

"She just found the mess," he said, stepping nimbly out of the way as Meredith shot past him, calling ahead to Consuella in perfectly accented Spanish.

"Quite a mornin', ain't it, Rich?" Loren grinned as he took his cigarettes out of his shirt pocket. "Can't remember when I've heard s'much screamin' before breakfast."

He shook out a cigarette for himself, lit it, then offered the pack and his lighter to Richard. What Richard wanted was a drink, a double anything, but he settled for a smoke, inhaling gratefully as he handed Loren's silver windproof lighter back to him.

"I quit cigarettes four years ago," he admitted, "but yesterday I bought and smoked a whole pack."

"Well, son—" Loren put on his hat, tugged the curled, sweat-stained brim over his eyes "—it's been my experience that tryin' t'keep your juice bottled up'll do all manner of strange things to a fella."

Richard choked as he inhaled. Throat burning with trapped smoke, he turned away from Loren, coughing and wheezing like a wind-broken horse.

"Strange how it happens sometimes," Loren went on, while Richard did his best not to strangle. "I've actually seen stallions go plum crazy if they don't get a mare."

"You're joking," Richard gasped, managing to draw a breath.

"'Fraid not. Had to put down a couple of 'em. Damn near killed the mares once they got to 'em. Time'r two thought I'd have t'take my .45 to ol' Flagmaster, but Susie managed to calm him down."

"You have my word, Loren," Richard croaked, wiping away the tears streaming from his eyes, "I won't go plum crazy."

"Mighty glad t'hear it, son. Mighty glad. Reckon you got fine sap in you." Loren gave him a clap on the shoulder that nearly knocked him off his feet. "Be a cryin' damn shame to have to shoot you."

10

PEEKING THROUGH the screen door—all the better to eavesdrop, my dear—Meredith cringed as Loren cracked Richard on the back and sent him stumbling toward a redwood chaise. Easing the inside door shut, she leaned her forehead against it and said under her breath, "Damn."

Nothing was going right today. She'd hurt Susan's feelings, her wedding was a disaster, and if she didn't do something fast there'd be a funeral in the family. It wasn't *all* Richard's fault, but he'd started it when he'd failed to recognize Susan, and compounded it when he'd tried to seduce her in the middle of the living room. The idiot.

When Susan came home from the restaurant in a teary rage sans Richard, Meredith had taken up a strategic position in the shadowy living-room alcove where her grandmother's cherry spinet sat between corner bookshelves. Armed with a stack of holiday sheet music and an alibi about practicing before the Rainbow's End Christmas party, which no one who'd ever heard her play would question, she'd been about to step forward to suggest they adjourn to the boudoir when Loren came through the back door.

Long ago Meredith had learned to be prepared when it came to Richard. The one thing she hadn't planned on was Loren Cade's on-the-spot transformation into an overprotective father. He'd always liked Richard, or seemed to, until now. She wasn't sure if the problem was Susan, something else, or a combination of the two.

Was it possible, Meredith wondered, that Loren had realized what she'd long known about Richard—that he was his own worst enemy, that just when you thought he had it all together he'd drop something? And probably break it. Something as fragile, perhaps, as his daughter's heart.

If so, she decided, they were all in big trouble.

At Foxglove, her mother still kept Richard's favorite coffee mug for him. Hand-painted sausages wearing straw hats, spats and carrying canes, danced above the caption, "Hope for the best but expect the wurst." It summed up Richard's outlook on life, explained why he always ended up with the short straw. He expected it—and so he got it.

But not this time. No sirree Bob. Not if Meredith had anything to do with it. This time, come hell or high water, Richard was going to come out on top. The winner. The hero carried off the field. The guy who kisses the girl at the end. If it killed him. Preferably before Loren Cade did.

Nudging the inside door open, Meredith saw her uncle strolling across the lawn toward the barns. She saw Richard, too, pushing up the sleeves of his sweater and fisting his hands as he started after him. The John Wayne swagger in his stride shot a jolt of alarm up her back. Grabbing the white box she'd stuffed the remnants of the veil into, Meredith pushed through the screen door.

"Hey, Richard!"

He swung halfway around to face her on the flagstone path. With his hair glinting in the bright morning sun he looked as if he'd just stepped off Mount Olympus; a Greek god with a muscle twitching in his jaw, madder than hell.

"I need a chauffeur," Meredith said, "and somebody to bail me out of jail."

"Why? Are you planning to kill somebody, too?"

"No. I'm going to take this veil back to Phillipe, the dim-witted designer who made it and tried to tell me on the phone I ordered winter white in the first place."

"You can't return pieces, can you?"

"No. But I can stuff them one at a time down Phillipe's throat until he chokes."

Richard glanced over his shoulder at Loren's retreating figure. Meredith thought fast.

"Then I plan to drop by Roundhouse and tell Luke we're eloping."

Richard swung fully around to face her. His fingers relaxed, slowly, but completely. So did Meredith.

"Roundhouse," he said. "Isn't that where Susan works?"

"Yes," she replied, thanking God he remembered.

"I'll get my jacket."

Five minutes later they were on their way into Santa Barbara, Richard behind the wheel of the BMW, Meredith belted into the passenger seat. His left arm was stretched on the door, a pensive half frown on his face. The sunroof was open, his wondrously blond hair fluttering like spun silver around the tortoiseshell frames of his sunglasses.

Meredith could just see his heart-stopping profile in the bottom left corner of the rearview mirror. She still couldn't quite believe this gorgeous hunk was the four-eyed geek she'd grown up with. She'd never understood what Susan saw in Richard, and wondered if the body snatchers had invaded England. Or if Susan, by virtue of her gift, had been able to look into the future and see his potential.

Phillipe's receptionist certainly had no trouble recognizing it. Her blue eyes turned misty as a Johnny Mathis song when Richard came through the boutique doors behind her.

"Oh, Miss Parker-Harris. Is this—your fiancé?"

The oh-God-if-he-is-I'll-slit-my-wrists catch in her voice made Meredith smile and think briefly about saying yes—until she remembered how desperately she needed a veil.

"No, Roxanne. This is my brother, Richard."

"Oh how *nice*." She rose from her chair, tossing her waist-length blond hair over one shoulder. In a white minidress that clung to her beach-bronzed curves, she looked like a living, breathing suntan-lotion ad. "I mean," she said, aiming a megawatt smile at Richard, "how nice to meet you."

"Hello." He nodded politely, the preoccupied, almost-but-not-quite frown still on his face.

Folding his sunglasses into the breast pocket of his tan corduroy blazer, he ambled away from the desk toward a rack of frothy bridesmaid dresses, bored but doing his best to hide it. And completely oblivious, Meredith realized. Not only to Roxanne but the impression he'd made on her.

It wasn't possible. No one with a face and physique like Richard's could be unaware of its effect on the opposite sex. He couldn't be that obtuse. Or insecure. Could he?

"You and Roxanne have something in common," Meredith said. "She was Phi Beta Kappa at Cal State. You were Phi Beta Kappa at Princeton."

Roxanne aimed another blinding, I'm-yours-for-the-asking smile at Richard. He looked over his shoulder, said, "Oh really," and turned back to the dresses.

"She only works here part-time," Meredith went on. "Roxanne is a graduate student. In ar-chi-tec-ture."

She said the word slowly, enunciating all four syllables. Richard glanced at her with a vague smile. "Challenging field," he said, turning to face her in front of a wall display. He cleared his throat and arched an eyebrow at the veils pinned to faceless plastic foam heads behind him.

"Tough luck," Meredith said under her breath to Roxanne, then loud enough for Richard to hear, "I want to see Phillipe."

"I'm sorry, Miss Parker-Harris," Roxanne replied sulkily, "but you know he sees clients only by appointment."

"Fine." Meredith put the white box on the desk and took off the lid. "Then you can give him this."

Roxanne peered inside and asked, "What is it?"

"A veil. Phillipe made it but I didn't order it." Meredith withdrew a copy of the original invoice from her shoulder bag and handed it to Roxanne. "I ordered an ivory veil. It says so right here."

Roxanne read the slip and gave it back. "So it does. Just a moment," she said and turned away from the desk.

She walked the way she looked, as if she'd been born in a bikini on a sun-drenched beach. Meredith glanced sideways at Richard. He was stifling a yawn and looking at his watch.

"Are you wearing your contacts?" she asked.

"Of course I am. Why d'you keep asking me that?"

"You look tired. Didn't you sleep well?"

"I have jet lag, Meredith. My biological clock has lost nine hours in the past four days."

A door at the back of the shop opened. Phillipe came through it, but not voluntarily. Roxanne was behind him, pushing. His feet were dug into the plush pink carpet to resist, hers to shove harder—until Phillipe saw Richard.

It was love at first sight—glazed eyes, quavering lower lip, thudding pulse at the base of his throat. Susan had told Meredith she'd looked the same way the first time she'd seen Luke. Not that he'd been much to look at then with his chubby round face and eyelashes so pale you could hardly see them. At fourteen, Meredith realized, Luke had looked remarkably like Phillipe.

His hands in his trouser pockets, Richard turned away from the veil display. When he saw Roxanne and Phillipe, his eyebrow shot up another notch.

"Don't tell me," the pudgy little designer said faintly. "This is your fiancé."

"No, Phillipe. My brother, Richard."

"*Wonderful!*" Unlooping the tape measure hung around his neck, he came bounding toward Richard in purple hightop Reeboks. "You're in the wedding party, aren't you? The best man *obviously*. And a thirty-two long or I'm no judge of—"

"Hold it." Richard held up his right hand. No more than eight inches shy of his inseam, Phillipe came to a toe-stubbing halt. "I'm a thirty-four."

"The story of my life," Phillipe sighed, draping his tape around his neck as he turned toward Meredith. "So show me this invoice that supposedly says ivory tulle."

"It doesn't *supposedly* say it," she retorted, producing the slip from her purse again. "It says it, *period*."

"Well obviously," Phillipe replied, giving the copy a quick scan, "it's a mistake."

"No. *This* is a mistake." Meredith grabbed the box off Roxanne's desk and upended it, showering Phillipe's purple feet with shredded tulle. "Or should I say was?"

"That was very mean of you, Meredith." Phillipe thrust his hands on his hips and tapped his foot, sending little puffs of tulle fluttering. "I suppose you expect me to make you another one."

"You bet I do. In *ivory* tulle. To match the dress you finished making for me a month ago."

"I can't possibly. There simply isn't enough time. I did you a favor working you into my schedule as it was, but now, after this—" Phillipe shrugged and stuck his bottom lip out petulantly "—I'm afraid I'm just not in the mood."

"Is that so?" Meredith smiled and folded her arms. "Do the initials IRA have any meaning for you?"

Phillipe's eyes narrowed. "You wouldn't dare."

"I'm getting married four weeks from tomorrow." Meredith tucked the invoice in her purse and snapped it shut. "If I don't have a veil, you will *never* own a villa in Acapulco."

Turning sharply on her heel, she headed for the door. Richard was already there, holding it open, the corners of his mouth twitching.

"That's blackmail!" Phillipe howled behind her.

"Call it what you want." Meredith turned halfway around in the doorway. "Make me a veil or I'll make you a pauper."

"Would you really?" Richard asked, pulling the door shut quickly behind them to drown out Phillipe's shrieks.

"No, sorely tempted though I am." Meredith closed her hand on her purse strap and pretended it was Phillipe's neck. "How in hell could he mistake white for ivory?"

"Maybe he's color-blind," Richard suggested, taking her keys out of his pocket as he steered her toward the car.

"Bite your tongue," Meredith snapped.

He pressed the disarm-and-lock pad on her key tab. The BMW hiccuped as the alarm disengaged, and so did Richard attempting to stifle a laugh behind the hand he swept over his mouth.

"Go ahead—laugh. It's my wedding, not yours."

He did laugh as he opened Meredith's door, shut it behind her, walked around the car and got in behind the wheel. "Sorry," he said with a grin. "But I wouldn't let a guy who wears purple tennis shoes design a bread wrapper."

"He has a hot-pink pair, too. And lime green."

"And you let him design your wedding dress?"

"Maybe you're right. Maybe he is color-blind."

They laughed together for the first time Meredith could remember. Richard used to laugh *at* her, and at Susan, too. Meredith had been a college sophomore in a prerequisite psychology course before she'd realized he treated them the way he'd been treated—belittled by Richard Senior, ridiculed by his mother and grandmother.

Poor Richard, Meredith thought. "Poor Phillipe," she said, as he backed the BMW out of its parking space, "I think he might've given up his purple Reeboks for you."

"Now, Meredith," Richard replied tolerantly, as he eased the BMW into the traffic on State Street. "To each his own."

"And Roxanne would have given you the dress off her back. Right there in the shop."

Richard gave her a dubious glance. "Not a chance."

"That's obviously what she thought. But if you'd given her the tiniest bit of encouragement, you could've had a walking, talking Barbie doll of your very own." She wagged her eyebrows at Richard as he braked at a stoplight and turned his head to look at her. "Trust me."

He gave her an amused half smile and shrugged. "Not my type," he said, and put on his sunglasses.

The light changed. So did the expression on Richard's face. The pensive frown came back as he accelerated through the intersection.

"What is your type?" Meredith asked.

"A week ago I would have told you blue-blooded blondes. Now I don't know."

Like Lady Alfreda, Meredith thought, watching Richard's frown deepen. She gripped her purse strap tighter, willing him to say leggy redheads, but he sighed instead and shook his head.

"I don't know much of anything, really." He bent his elbow on the door and ran his hand through his hair. "I'm beginning to wonder if I ever did."

Uh-oh, Meredith thought. Was this jet lag or anxiety? Richard had been prone to attacks the family doctor said were asthma, but the staff physician at the military academy Richard Senior had sent him to—to toughen him up, until Lady Simpson got a court order—said he was anxious, not asthmatic. "Anxious!" Richard Senior had bellowed at his son. "What the hell do you have to be anxious about?"

The medical report came home with Richard at Thanksgiving, the worst one Meredith could remember, and Susan's first at Foxglove. Twenty guests had come to dinner, an agony of too much rich food and frigid civility. In the middle of dessert, Richard had gotten sick all over the handwoven wool Oriental carpet.

Susan had burst into tears while Richard stood dry-eyed and white as the linen tablecloth. At ten o'clock that night Susan was still crying. Meredith had thrown a pillow at her and told her to shut up so she could sleep. "I'm not the one who's crying!" she'd sobbed. "Richard is!"

Only he wasn't, Meredith had discovered, at least not visibly, when she marched down the hall to tell him to knock it off. His bedroom was dark except for a beam of bitter moonlight pooling on the bed where he sat, stone-faced and dry-eyed, his back against the wall and his arms locked around a pillow.

"Susan told me you were crying," she said.

"Susan's nuts," he replied. "I never cry."

The next morning he'd gone back to school, three days early. Meredith wondered if Richard still didn't cry and if he still hated turkey.

"Uh-oh," she said, opening her purse and digging through it. "Don't tell me I forgot Consuella's list. I don't see it. Do you? It's written in Spanish on—"

"The back of a blue envelope?" Richard asked, plucking one from the map pocket on the door.

"That's it. Thank God I didn't forget it."

Richard glanced at the list, handed it to her and asked, "What's *pavo*?"

"Turkey," Meredith replied, tucking the envelope in her purse.

"None for me, thanks. I hate turkey."

"I know, Richard, but tomorrow is Thanksgiving."

11

And barely a month after that was Meredith's wedding on Christmas Eve. Which gave Richard four weeks—exactly twenty-nine days—to get his act together.

One for every year of his life, he thought. It was ironic as hell, probably no more than he deserved, and definitely not enough time for a guy who'd just realized he hated colored underwear to figure out where he'd zigged when he should've zagged and get his life back on track.

Not that he'd be thrown out with the wrapping paper on Christmas morning, but since he'd come to Cicada Ranch to attend Meredith's wedding, on or shortly after December twenty-sixth he'd have to go. The burning question was where. That it was the same burning question he'd wakened to in New York did not escape him.

His grand plan had seemed so simple on the plane with a Bloody Mary in his hand: take Susan to the track, make a killing at the twenty-dollar window, dance with Meredith at her wedding, and split. Instead, he'd insulted Susan, not once but twice, and made an enemy of Loren Cade. Maybe he *had* killed one brain cell too many.

He'd been so sure Susan owed him, so convinced it was the least she could do. Now he was sure of only one thing. If he didn't get a drink in the next five minutes, the balloon swelling inside his chest, the one rapidly filling with long-suppressed anger, was going to explode. Giving Meredith a smile he said, "Let me buy you lunch."

Ten minutes later they were seated at a table in a trendy Mexican bistro near West Beach. Richard ordered a pitcher of margaritas and drank two in the time it took Meredith to squeeze lemon into her iced tea. Halfway through the meal, he flagged the waiter for another. When it came, Meredith leaned back in her chair and looked at him over their enchilada platters.

"You're putting away margaritas the way your grandmother puts away highballs."

"An old shrew, my Gram," he said cheerfully, "but she can sure hold her liquor."

"She's an old drunk, Richard."

"You bet." He grinned at her and refilled his glass. "But she's a damn good one."

The tequila had done its job, pricked a slow leak in the balloon. He felt relaxed and in control, at the top of his form. So what if he was captain of a ship with no rudder? Once he had a few bucks in his pocket, he'd buy one.

"I'd like to leave now, please." Meredith laid her napkin on the table, picked up her purse and rose.

Richard gulped the last of his drink, tossed two twenties on the table and followed her outside. The sea breeze rustling the palms along the beach, the sand glittering in the sun, gave him a rush of peace and well-being. What a beautiful place. He felt safe here, sheltered from life's storms, like the Channel Islands sheltered the city and the harbor from the storms of the Pacific.

The thought was a cliché, but one of his better ones. Pleased with it, Richard smiled, put on his shades and took Meredith's car keys out of his pocket. She snatched them out of his hand and said, as she stalked past him, "I'll drive."

"It's your car," he replied mildly, ambling toward the passenger side, "but I'm perfectly fine. Look." Catching her eye over the yellow roof of the BMW, he stretched his arms out, bent his elbows and touched the tip of his nose with his index fingers three times. "See?"

"You do that very well." Meredith gave him a sour look over the rims of her sunglasses. "Had a lot of practice?"

Richard laughed, slid into the car and fastened his seat belt. Meredith got in behind the wheel and slammed her door so hard the BMW rocked on its springs.

"Great enchiladas." Richard sighed, crossing his ankles and his arms. "Best I've had since I went to England."

"How would you know?" Meredith tossed her purse on the seat between them and started the engine. "You hardly touched yours."

"I ate until I was full," he replied, turning his head to look at her as she backed the BMW out of its parking space. "How do you think I keep my girlish figure?"

"People who've been drinking shouldn't drive, and people who love them don't let them," Meredith retorted, threading the BMW through the parking lot toward the exit. "Even Uncle Loren never drove when he was drinking."

"Oh come off it. The man was never sober."

"He is now and has been for five years."

"Well bully for him."

"He learned a lot about himself at the clinic. Like why he started drinking in the first place." Meredith braked at the exit, wrapped her hands around the top of the steering wheel and looked at him. "Cowboys don't cry, they drink. They don't talk about their feelings, they drown them."

"In Oplahoma, anyway." When Meredith slid her sunglasses down her nose and glared at him, Richard said with a grin, "It's a joke, step-brat."

"It's not funny. It never was." Meredith trod on the gas, squealing the tires as she pulled out onto Cabrillo Boulevard. "So tell me, Richard, when was the last time you had a good cry?"

Meredith, like Bea and the elephants, never forgot anything. His stepmother always remembered his birthday, sent him cards at Easter and Valentine's Day. She'd also been witness to his most towering humiliations, but unlike her daughter, she had grace and breeding enough not to mention them.

"Just this morning as a matter of fact," he retorted coldly, "when I cut myself shaving."

"Liar," Meredith shot back. "You've never shed a tear in your life. Not even when Susan broke your nose."

He'd wanted to then. Oh God, how he'd wanted to. He couldn't remember the pain, but in his dreams he sometimes saw the look of utter disgust on his father's face when he'd pulled him off the back of Meredith's horse.

"I'm sorry," she said, turning north on Highway 101, "I'm having a lousy day and I'm taking it out on you."

"Quite all right," Richard replied shortly. "I'm not exactly having a red-letter one myself."

And what about Susan? What kind of day was she having? Richard wondered about it, but not for long. Jet lag, not tequila, caught up with him as the Beemer hummed down the highway. He fell asleep and dreamed about Susan instead, jerky, fitful pictures of her in the emerald-green dress, wading toward him across a straw-heaped stall, a come-hither smile on her face, then stabbing a pitchfork into a hay-bale effigy of him. Right in the groin. That woke him up, as his chin thudded onto his chest and the Beemer made a sweeping turn between massive stone gate posts. Overhead a white iron arch spelled Roundhouse Stables.

Good thing, too, otherwise Richard might've thought he was on the Ponderosa. Pastures as green as Susan's dress, bound by white rail fences connected by posts topped with carriage lamps, stretched as far as he could see. Twenty-five-mile-an-hour speed limit and cleverly designed Horse Crossing signs edged the road; the road to Zanzibar, striped down the middle with a yellow no-passing line, winding past barn after barn and paddock after paddock dotted with grazing Thoroughbreds.

"Good lord," Richard said. "This place makes Foxglove look like a tenant farm."

"It is a bit overwhelming the first time," Meredith said. "That's why I brought you in the side gate."

The side gate. Holy God. Richard wiped a hand over his mouth and looked at Meredith. "And you're marrying this?"

"No," she replied sharply, "I'm marrying the man who owns it."

Same difference, Richard thought, but didn't say so. Instead he looked out the side window at what was clearly a multimillion-dollar operation and asked, "What happens to Cicada once you're queen of all this?"

"Nothing happens to it. Cicada belongs to Susan. She bought me out a year ago."

A year ago Richard had bought Serena, the chestnut voyeur, for Alfreda. And a Cartier watch. Susan had bought a ranch. With a house on it she could live in, with food in it she could eat.

"Her salary must be on par with the surroundings," he said, hoping his voice didn't sound as small as he felt.

"I found some very lucky and very lucrative investments for her, too." Meredith bent her left elbow on the door and glanced at him. "How's your portfolio, by the way?"

Richard almost laughed. It was that or cry, but he'd forgotten how, if he'd ever known. He wished he could.

He tried to remember what had moved him to tears in New York, but that portion of his memory was nothing but a blank. Maybe that was the brain cell he'd killed.

"Just fine," he lied, shaking his head. "I can't wait to see what he gives you for a wedding present."

"I know what I want. Would you like to see?"

"Why not," he replied dully.

Meredith turned into a small paved lot next to a white barn the size of an auditorium and parked next to Susan's Blazer. Richard got out of the BMW like an old man. He felt like one, too, washed-up, used-up, finished before he'd even started. On and off all day he'd ached to see Susan, now he wasn't sure what he'd do or say if he did.

"Susan probably isn't here," Meredith said, as they walked toward the barn, "but she always parks here."

It was Richard's first break of the day, and the way things were going, probably his last. The double-width barn doors looked too big to budge and as heavy as the depression seeping through him, but the right one slid smoothly open on a well-oiled track.

Richard followed Meredith inside and shut the door with a solid thud. Aristocratic equine heads swung in their direction over polished oak half doors, the sun slanting through the windows under the eaves splashing puddles of light on their burnished coats and the smoothly raked loam floor.

Drawing a breath remarkably short on horse smell and long on clean, sweet straw, Richard folded his sunglasses into his pocket and followed Meredith down the row. In front of a stall about two-thirds of the way along she stopped.

"Here she is," she said almost reverently. "Her name is High Brow."

Richard's first glimpse over the stall door made his breath catch. He'd seen a lot of Thoroughbreds in his lifetime, frankly more than he'd ever cared to, but never one as exquisite as this.

She was big for a filly, about sixteen and one-half hands, all legs and lung room. Her coat was a vivid chestnut, almost but not quite as bright as a new penny. It gleamed and rippled with muscle as she stamped a hoof and buried her nose deeper in her grain box.

"She's Luke's pride and joy," Meredith said. "The best Roundhouse has ever bred. Isn't she's gorgeous?"

"Magnificent comes closer," Richard murmured.

He spoke hardly above a whisper, but High Brow, who'd been ignoring them so far, abruptly lifted her nose and swung her head toward them. She had a narrow white blaze, so perfectly shaped it looked painted on, and the longest, thickest eyelashes Richard had ever seen on a horse. Her eyes were large, very dark and well spaced.

One at a time her ears flicked forward and her nostrils flared. When her ears went flat against her head, Meredith tugged Richard back a step.

"She's very high-strung and shy," she whispered, "and she doesn't know you."

For the first time in his life, Richard wished he had a carrot in his pocket. No, an apple, a Jonathan, or maybe a Granny Smith. High Brow looked like the apple type.

The filly lowered her head, her nostrils flaring wider as she came toward them. Meredith moved closer, thinking she was coming to her, the scent she knew. So did Richard, until High Brow stretched her head over the stall door and lipped the front of his sweater.

He was amazed—that she didn't use her teeth and that he didn't jump out of his clothes. He'd been known to run screaming from Thoroughbreds half her size. Instead he raised his right hand, cupped her muzzle, and felt a jolt of sensation prickle the nape of his neck.

It reminded him of Bea's gentle touch against his cheek, as she bent over him in his room at Foxglove, checking to make sure he was tucked in and covered, as she always did on her way to bed. That's what it felt like—a warm, dreamy jolt, like being startled while still half-asleep.

"I don't believe it," Meredith said. "She likes you."

"Amazing as it seems, that happens sometimes."

High Brow snorted and butted his chest with her nose.

"Correct me if I'm wrong," he said, "but won't High Brow be as much yours as she is Luke's the second you say I do?"

"Yes, but I have plans for her."

"What plans?"

"Promise you won't tell?"

"Word of honor."

"I'm going to give her to Susan for Christmas."

If she'd said she wanted to sell High Brow for dog food, Richard couldn't have been more surprised. Meredith hadn't been out in the sun, she hadn't drunk any margaritas. Clearly she was nuts. But just to make sure, he asked, "Are you nuts?"

"No." Meredith smiled and moved closer to stroke High Brow's sleek neck. "But Luke will think I am. That's why I'm not telling him."

"I'd suggest you never tell him, but sooner or later he's bound to notice the empty stall."

"Oh, I intend to tell him. At the reception, in front of Mother and Daddy and three hundred wedding guests. That way he can't kill me. Or renege later."

Richard was right. She was nuts. But he didn't say so. Instead he said, "That's very generous of you, Meredith."

"No, it's very selfish. High Brow has the potential to found a tremendous bloodline once she's finished racing." Her hand went still on the filly's neck as she looked steadily at Richard. "That's one of Susan's dreams, and I want her to have it. She has other dreams, too, but barring a miracle, High Brow may be the only one I'm able to give her."

The filly snorted again and shook her head. Richard felt another zip up his spine, rubbed the back of his neck and felt sweat. It was warm in here, that's what was wrong with him. Too damn warm and getting warmer by the second. That's why he felt disjointed, almost out of focus.

"Dreams don't do you much good if they don't come true now and then," Meredith continued, rubbing High Brow's neck, her voice sounding tinny over the dull roar starting in Richard's ears. "I just want to help Susan's along a little bit. I just want her to be happy."

What Richard wanted was out of here, out of the refracted sunlight beating down on his head and the heat thrown off by the stabled horses, away from the headache clustering at the base of his skull. He'd had too much tequila on a nearly empty stomach, too much of Meredith and her goody-two-shoes impulses.

"I believe in dreams," she said, "don't you?"

"I don't know. I've never—"

Had any, he meant to say, until High Brow swung her head around and fixed an eye on him. One very large and very dark eye, except for a tiny speck of diamond brightness in the center that snagged his consciousness. He forgot what he meant to say as colors he'd never seen before burst inside his head: blinding blue, a green so vivid it vibrated. There were images inside the colors, but he couldn't make them out. He sensed them, but only for a flash, a heartbeat.

They shattered when the barn door opened, turned to smoke and straw dust in a shaft of sunlight that shot like a spear down the corridor. With a startled whinny, High Brow threw up her head and wheeled away from him.

Richard felt, almost heard, a snap in the back of his head and nearly crumpled like a marionette whose strings had been cut. If he hadn't grabbed the stall door he would have, but Meredith didn't see, thank God. She was looking past him, starting down the row with a bright-eyed smile.

"Luke, darling! Great news. Phillipe screwed up my veil and doesn't have time to make another one, so we're eloping."

"Sorry, cutie, no can do. Aunt Phyllis is coming from 'Frisco expecting a wedding. If she doesn't get one I'll get hell."

Cutie? Oh Christ. No wonder he couldn't remember Seth Hardin's boy. Luke had never called Meredith anything but cutie, and Richard had rarely called *him* anything but Lumpy; sometimes Tub-o—short for Tub-o-Guts—or Doughboy, an interesting double entendre, since his father made Richard Senior look like a pauper. Until the day Luke had had enough, threw Richard on the ground and sat on his chest until black spots swam in front of him.

They'd hated each other, for no particular reason. Never as quick or as glib, but always about twenty pounds heavier and ten times sneakier than Richard, Lumpy had been an expert at killer noogies on a staircase, clotheslines as he came around a corner and kidney punches nobody ever saw.

"Well, well, if it isn't my old buddy Four Eyes," Lumpy Hardin said. "How's it going?"

Richard cringed and doubled a fist on the stall door. He hated being called Four Eyes as much as Luke hated Lumpy. Taking a deep breath and squaring his shoulders, he turned around.

For a moment all he could see was Susan, walking beside Hardin, leading the fattest, ugliest black Shetland pony he'd ever seen. Her head was bowed, her hair glowing like a sunset in the light spilling through the open door behind her. Richard wanted to touch it but dragged his gaze away from her, focused on Hardin and almost grabbed the stall door again.

Bea had told him Luke would grow into his baby fat someday and then he'd be sorry. Oh boy, was she right. Oh boy, was he sorry. He'd grown into it all right, all the way up to six-three, maybe four. Meredith looked like a munchkin tucked beneath his left arm. Susan still looked at the floor.

To meet Hardin's eye, Richard had to raise his chin just a hair. When he did, Luke came to an abrupt stop about three feet shy of High Brow's stall. Oddly, he looked as startled as Richard felt. Beside him, Susan tugged the pony to a halt, her eyes lifting a fraction.

"Just fine, Lumpy," Richard said. "How's by you?"

Susan's chin shot up, her eyes simmering. The ugly black pony laid back his ears and rumbled in his chest.

"Well, at last," she snapped, "you remember *somebody*."

12

OF COURSE she had to say it standing next to Luke, the worst person in the world to make a crack like that in front of, except Meredith. When would she learn? Susan thought, with a groan.

"What's that, Suz?" Luke snapped his head around to look at her, a grin on his face, a gleam in his eye. "Old Four Eyes didn't know you from Adam? Or should I say Eve?"

"Something like that," she said, tightening her grip on Satan's lead as the pony shifted restlessly.

"Poor Suz. That must've been a swift kick in the—*ow!*" Luke howled, as Satan trod on his right foot.

"Thank you," Susan muttered into the pony's cupped ear, "but I can handle this myself."

Satan rolled an eye at her and snorted.

Leaning on Meredith, Luke hopped on his left foot and sucked air between his teeth. It was tough, but Susan managed not to laugh. Luke should have known better than to take pot shots at her in front of Satan, especially when he was out of his stall. She was one of the few people the old bugger had a soft spot for in his black-as-his-hide heart.

Richard, however, didn't even try to conceal his amusement. He stood with his arms folded, grinning ear to ear.

When his gaze shifted toward Susan she looked quickly away, clucked to Satan, and tugged him toward the stall he shared with High Brow. She could just see Richard in the corner of her eye and thought his grin dimmed a bit as he stepped out of her way, but wasn't sure.

High Brow came to the stall door. Just looking at her, wickering as she stretched her neck to touch noses with Satan, gave Susan a catch in her heart. Just like seeing Richard always did. She clamped down hard on the thought, but wasn't quick enough. Satan laid back his ears and rumbled, and High Brow tossed up her head and whinnied at Richard.

Even though it wasn't directed at her, Susan felt the jolt up her spine all the way down her arms. It left her fingertips tingling and her breath trapped in her throat as she spun on her heel toward Richard. He was rubbing the back of his neck and grimacing like he had a headache. One hell of a headache.

Which he would if High Brow was sending and he wasn't receiving. Once or twice as a child, before realizing her link with horses worked both ways, Susan had almost been knocked flat. The younger the horse, the more powerful the send. Adolescents like High Brow were especially excitable and had a tendency to overdo it when they found an empathic human.

Remembering the yellow rose and Richard's certainty that it was her favorite gave Susan another shock. There went her theory that he'd guessed or Meredith had told him. He'd *known*, all right, just as High Brow *knew*.

Richard lowered his hand, lifted his head, and locked his gaze with hers. Caught off guard, Susan couldn't pull back quickly enough to avoid a second of connection with him. Richard couldn't receive but he could send and relay, like a microwave tower bounced a signal. He passed High Brow's vibrant essence to her on a beam of raw longing. It was and it wasn't the same old need Susan had always sensed in him, because now she understood it and its source.

Still, she turned her back on him and lifted the latch on the stall door. It was the quickest, surest way to sever the link. High Brow backed obediently away, the glorious shade of pink, her signature color, fading inside Susan's head as she unhooked the lead from Satan's halter and turned him into the stall.

"That's the ugliest pony I've ever seen," Richard said, coming up beside her. "Not to mention the fattest."

"Watch how you toss that word around, Four Eyes." Luke managed to straighten, gingerly, on his right foot and square off on Richard.

"I will if you will." Richard leaned his left hand on the stall door and curled his right one, resting on his hip, into a fist. "Lumpy."

"Maybe you oughta break out your old Coke-bottle lenses." Luke lifted his arm from Meredith's shoulders. "Maybe then you'd be able to recognize people you've known half your life."

"I wear contacts now."

Luke slapped his hand against his flat, trim abdomen. "Thirty-two-inch waist, Four Eyes."

Richard tapped his temple. "Twenty-twenty, Lumpy."

"Before one of you reaches for his zipper," Meredith said tartly, stepping between them, "I think we should call a truce. Don't you, Susan?"

"I think it's time I went home," she said, glancing at her watch. Three-thirty, her usual quitting time. This had been the shortest, yet one of the longest days of her life. "I'll work up a diet for Tub—er—Satan," she told Luke. "If you can't find a groom brave enough to exercise him, let me know. I'll send Rufus over."

"I'll do it myself if I have to," Luke replied. "I feel awful about this. I had no idea he was so overweight."

"Who does that surprise?" Richard muttered behind her.

"I didn't, either, till I got a good look at him last Sunday," Susan replied, ignoring Richard. "We'll slim him down, don't worry. See you in the morning."

Swiftly she started down the row. She had three hours of paperwork and four hours of chores waiting for her at Cicada. And a lot to think about. She had no idea Richard was right behind her until she reached out to grab the door and pull it shut behind her. When his fingers closed over hers on the handle, she started, tried to pull away, but couldn't. His grip tightened just enough to hold her.

"Can we talk?" he asked, his breath wafting across her cheek as she glanced back at him.

Susan's heart wrenched. Either his after-shave was eighty proof or he'd been drinking. Yanking her hand free, she slid sideways through the door.

"Sure, when you're sober," she said over her shoulder, turning away and making quick tracks for her Blazer.

Richard followed her, but Susan expected it. What she didn't expect was the anger blazing across his face when he caught her left elbow and spun her around. His cheeks were flushed with it, his eyes narrowed.

"I had a couple margaritas at lunch. That doesn't make me a drunk."

"I didn't say you were a drunk. I said you'd been drinking."

He blinked, startled and thrown off balance. The advantage was hers and Susan pressed it.

"You're awfully defensive for a guy who isn't a drunk," she said, lifting her elbow out of his hand. "I think you ought to ask yourself why."

Then she bolted for the truck. Susan wanted to put as much distance between them as fast as she could. She'd been this close to Richard before when he was this upset and knew what was coming. Still it almost staggered her when it hit, a wave of pain and anger, laced with the crushing loneliness Susan had never understood until now.

Now, everything was clear to her. At last, all the complex pieces of Richard fit together—his drinking, his loathing of horses, the mask he hid behind. Gripping the door handle of the Blazer, Susan gritted her teeth and waited for the onslaught to pass.

When it did, she dug her keys out of her pocket, yanked the door open, gripped the steering wheel and hauled herself up behind the wheel. With shaky fingers she started the engine, shoved the truck in reverse and backed up, then shifted into drive and shot out of the car park in a squeal of rubber.

She kept to the speed limit on the Roundhouse road, but floored the accelerator when she hit the county blacktop. Her insides were shaking along with her hands, but she didn't dare stop for fear she'd go back. That wouldn't solve anything. Not yet, and maybe not ever.

She should have *known,* should have realized years ago why she could pick up Richard's feelings so consistently and so accurately. He was just like her, an empath, possibly a telepath. It was no more possible to label him than it was to label herself. From experience Susan knew psychic talents overlapped, flowed from one into the other. For simplicity's sake, she referred to her gift as telepathy, though she suspected all psychically gifted people were first and foremost strong empaths.

Maybe if she hadn't fallen in love with Richard so long ago, she would have recognized his gift. Or maybe that's why she loved him. God knew. Susan didn't.

All she knew for sure was that something had happened to Richard since breakfast. Some kind of crisis had broken through his dam of defenses and denial. That was typically the case, she knew, from the research she'd done on her own on ESP. Horses were telepathic, any horseman worth his oats knew that. But no one seemed to know about empathic humans with the ability to read their minds. Susan had never found another documented case like hers, and suspected that most people with her ability chose a path similar to Richard's—they buried it and tried to pretend it didn't exist.

Remembering the turmoil she'd sensed along with the disjointed piano music, Susan guessed his breakup with Lady Alfreda was probably the catalyst, but not the cause of Richard's crisis. She suspected a combination of factors, but felt no real desire to find out what they were.

What mattered was how Richard would deal with his newly discovered sensitivity—if he was even aware of it. And based on what she'd witnessed in the barn, Susan was willing to bet he hadn't a clue.

Almost more than she wanted to draw her next breath, she wanted to drive back to Roundhouse, ask Richard if he had a headache, and if he said yes tell him why. But she had no right. Any interference would be the worst kind of manipulation. But God how she wanted to, how she wanted to use their shared empathic ability to bind Richard to her. It would be so easy. And so wrong.

Just when you thought life couldn't get any more complicated, it did. Susan bent her left elbow on the door, splayed her fingers on her temple and blinked back tears.

Oh wonderful, she remembered. Tomorrow was Thanksgiving.

13

OH WONDERFUL . . . tomorrow was Thanksgiving. . . .

The thought woke Richard with a start in the front seat of the BMW. It echoed through his head like a murmur in a seashell, a voice in a dream, only he couldn't remember dreaming. Hell, he couldn't even remember falling asleep.

"Did you say something?" he asked Meredith, blinking as he turned his head to look at her behind the wheel.

"No, but I'd like to now that you're awake," she said, glancing at him with a frown. "You behaved like a jerk."

"So did Lumpy." Richard yawned and rubbed the back of his neck where the killer headache he'd had when he'd fallen asleep still throbbed. That would teach him to nod off in a car with his head scrunched against the window twice in the same day. "And furthermore, he started it."

"That's not even an excuse, let alone a reason. It's a stupid macho rationalization. We were raised better than that, Richard."

"Maybe you were."

"I think you owe Luke an apology."

"The hell I do."

"He certainly won't apologize."

"So I should." Richard looked at her. "Is that it?"

"To avoid a food fight at dinner tomorrow, yes."

"Not a problem. I won't be joining you. I hate turkey, remember?"

"I've never asked you for anything, Richard."

"You want to blow your perfect record now?"

"If it will keep peace until my wedding, yes. I'm at my wit's end. Everything that possibly could has gone wrong."

"Maybe you should give serious thought to an elopement."

"Don't tempt me and don't change the subject."

"I will not apologize for something I didn't start."

"What would a handshake cost you?"

"What would it cost Lumpy?"

"*Luke,*" Meredith corrected him sharply. "The man who can get along with anyone. Anyone in the world. Except you."

"Put that one away, Meredith. It's beneath you."

"It's the truth. And it's not just Luke. Susan is furious because you stood her up last night and just this morning—in case you've forgotten, Mr. Congeniality—Uncle Loren threatened to shoot you."

"You eavesdropped!"

"Of course I did."

"You're the one who invited me here, Meredith." Richard felt the balloon swelling in his chest again. "You're the one who wouldn't take no for an answer."

"Maybe I wish I had."

"Fine. I'll leave."

"And go where?"

Good question. The frequency with which it kept popping up was beginning to piss Richard off.

"Tahiti, maybe. I've never been there."

"I don't want you to leave."

"Then what do you want?"

"I want you to apologize to Luke."

"When a Clydesdale wins the Kentucky Derby."

"A handshake never killed anybody." Meredith braked at a stop sign and glared at him. "You're behaving like a child."

"Really?" Richard arched an eyebrow at her. "And making confetti out of your wedding veil is mature, adult behavior?"

Meredith flushed, then stepped on the gas when the driver of the pickup truck behind them honked his horn.

"That's a completely different situation."

"Oh, naturally."

"I can't believe you're being so stubborn about such a small thing."

Neither could Richard. He couldn't believe he'd taken Lumpy's bait, that he'd argued twice with Susan since breakfast, that everyone else was having a lousy day, too. Maybe it was something in the stars. Or the pollen count.

"Believe it, Meredith. I am *not* going to apologize."

"Fine," she snapped. "Then don't."

"I won't," he snapped back, and turned his head to look out the side window.

Traffic was heavier, the two-lane blacktop widening to four as they neared civilization and the supermarket. It lay just ahead at one end of an adobe strip mall with a red tile roof. Holiday streamers festooned the parking lot, plastic bells thick with silver glitter swung from the light poles and flashed in the sun.

The glare shot like a hot needle straight to Richard's headache. He looked away, wincing, and lifting his sunglasses with his thumb and forefinger to pinch the bridge of his nose. Holy God what a headache. He felt queasy, turned his head toward Meredith to ask her to pull over before he lost his lunch, and saw her wipe a tear from her right cheek.

"Stop it this instant," he said in his harshest voice, his best imitation of Richard Senior. "Crybabies don't cut it."

It was his father's favorite catechism, the one Richard had heard most often growing up. So had Meredith.

"Don't quote Daddy to me," she shot back, tugging a tissue out of her purse on the seat between them. "He isn't here, so I don't have to be the perfect little soldier anymore. And neither do you, you dope. I'm a grown woman and I can damn well cry if I want."

The sob Meredith stifled closed like a vice on Richard's throat. There was something stuck there, just below his larynx. He tried to swallow it but couldn't, felt a clutch of panic and the clamp tighten as Meredith pinched the tissue over her nose.

"All right, goddammit, I'll apologize to Lumpy."

"Luke," she corrected him, sniffling as she eased the Beemer into the middle turn lane.

"Okay, okay—Luke. Just stop crying."

"Promise?" Meredith made a left into the parking lot and glanced at him with tear-misted eyes.

"Yes!" He all but shouted at her. "Now stop crying!"

She did, drawing and exhaling a deep, shaky breath. The vice relaxed and the balloon deflated, but his headache flared. Richard swallowed and closed his eyes. When the Beemer came to a stop he kicked his door open, jumped out of the car and sucked fresh air into his lungs.

What the hell was wrong with him? Why had he choked up like that? How had he known it wouldn't let up until Meredith stopped crying?

"Are you okay?" she asked, hooking her purse strap over her shoulder as she came around the car. "You look pale."

"I have a headache." Richard leaned his elbow on the roof of the Beemer and dragged his hand through his hair.

NO COST! NO OBLIGATION TO BUY!
NO PURCHASE NECESSARY!

> ...ache was gone. Snatching t...
> ...ard pressed the disarm, then sl...
> ...d. She didn't say anything, jus...
> ...his over with," he said, and st...

PLAY ''LUCKY 7''
AND GET AS MANY AS FIVE FREE GIFTS ...
HOW TO PLAY:

1. With a coin, carefully scratch off the silver box at the right. This makes you eligible to receive two or more free books, and possibly another gift, depending on what is revealed beneath the scratch-off area.

2. Send back this card and you'll receive brand-new Harlequin Temptation® novels. These books have a cover price of $2.99 each, but they are yours to keep absolutely free.

3. There's no catch. You're under no obligation to buy anything. We charge nothing—ZERO—for your first shipment. And you don't have to make any minimum number of purchases—not even one!

4. The fact is thousands of readers enjoy receiving books by mail from the Harlequin Reader Service®. They like the convenience of home delivery...they like getting the best new novels before they're available in stores ... and they love our discount prices!

5. We hope that after receiving your free books you'll want to remain a subscriber. But the choice is yours—to continue or cancel, anytime at all! So why not take us up on our invitation, with no risk of any kind. You'll be glad you did!

turkey, but that wasn't it at all. He hated Thanksgiving because it marked the beginning of the Christmas Season. And Richard hated Christmas almost as much as he hated horses.

It was a mistake to think about Christmas—it only attracted the spirit that came to haunt him every Yuletide, the Ghost of Christmas That Never Was. No matter where Richard went the specter found him, and sure enough appeared on cue to follow him into the shower. It glanced away in disgust at the tortured stirring the spray raised between his legs, but hovered behind him while he shaved, showing snapshots from its collection of the Merry Christmases in Richard's life.

The first Christmas after his parents' divorce, spent with his mother, was a memory of craning his neck to kiss her beneath a sprig of mistletoe in a doorway as she swept past, laughing, on Sir Freddie's arm. The ones with his grandmother and Aunt Agie were remembered as numbingly long afternoons after church spent wandering the Gramercy Park house while the two old dames slept off Cook's rum pudding in their armchairs. The best and the most bitter Christmases were passed at Foxglove, envying the warmth in Richard Senior's eyes as he watched Meredith and Susan shriek with glee over a new saddle or jodhpurs, the coolness in his gaze when his son unwrapped a chessboard.

Feel sheltered and protected here, do you? the spirit taunted. Finally found your place in the world, eh? Same day pigs fly, bucko.

"Shove it," Richard muttered, giving his jaw a too-hard slap of after-shave. "Sideways, pal."

But the spirit doggedly remained while he pulled on jeans and a navy cotton-knit sweater, trailed mournfully behind him when he left the guest room. At the juncture of the hallway and the living room, just this side of the kitchen archway, it jerked him around to face the Christmas tree towering in a far corner near the fireplace.

The reflections of its tiny blue lights flickered on the stone floor, the flames crackling behind the black mesh screen danced on its spun glass and crystal ornaments. The candles on the mantel filled the room with the scent of vanilla and bayberry, and Richard with an ache so sharp it snatched his breath.

The candles were the same colors, pale sage green and deep wine red, and the same scents Bea always burned on holidays. He stood there, awash in memory and misery, listening to pans clash in the kitchen, a scratchy voice humming above the hiss of running water. Consuella, not Bea. He was in California, not Virginia; at Cicada Ranch, not Foxglove Farm.

Tearing his gaze away from the tree, Richard wheeled through the archway into the kitchen. Saucepans bubbled on the stove, steaming the air and frizzing the ends of the dark braids wrapped around Consuella's head.

"Miss Meredith no here," she said, glancing at him from the corner sink where she stood peeling carrots. "You miss breakfast. No eat until dinner."

Richard's stomach growled mournfully. "Where is she?" he asked, though he couldn't have cared less.

Consuella turned back to the sink, flicking one hand irritably toward the window. Richard thought of Devlin, suppressed a burst of anger and an urge to snatch a carrot.

"Thank you. You've been very helpful," he said, exiting the house via the mudroom and the patio.

The BMW was parked next to Susan's Blazer, which meant Meredith was somewhere on the premises. And so was Susan. He hoped they weren't together. He had a few things to say to Susan, things best said in private. Richard struck off across the lawn toward the barns, the spirit tagging behind.

He wished he hadn't thought of Devlin and the old boy's unsolicited promise not to tell his grandmother where he'd gone. At the time Richard had been glad to have it, but now he wondered what would happen if his grandmother got tough and Devlin refused to talk. Would she fire him? The threat was nothing new. She fired Devlin a dozen times a day, but forgot when she sobered up.

What if this time she remembered? Richard would be responsible. He had no idea if Devlin had any savings or a pension, or that he'd covered so much ground until he stepped into the long, rectangular shadow cast by the foaling barn. Both doors were open, hinting that someone might be inside. Ideally someone with gloriously long legs, red hair and the wrong idea about him. An idea he intended to correct.

Sunbeams thick with straw dust slanted ahead of him as he started down the row past the bay mare and her two chestnut stablemates. They stretched their heads toward Richard as he passed, flared their nostrils but didn't wicker or whinny. He felt a twinge in the back of his neck, heard the rustle of straw ahead and the murmur of voices, but couldn't identify them until he neared the end of the corridor.

"I say tell him," Meredith said.

"I'd sooner have a root canal," Susan replied.

"At least you'd know."

"I think I've got a pretty good idea already."

"No you don't. You're just guessing."

"The hell I am."

"It's now or never, Susan."

"That's what you said last spring in London. Remember?"

Richard did, with a jolt that stopped him cold a foot shy of the corridor turn. The stall occupied by the bay mare with the swollen fetlock lay just around the right-hand corner. He tasted liniment on his tongue, remembered Meredith telling him she and Luke and Susan had been at Epsom. He remembered, too, the start her admission had given him, the oops-I-said-too-much wince in Meredith's expression.

"So I was wrong," she said. "So sue me. But this time I'm right. It's absolutely, positively *now* or never."

"Never, then."

"*Susan!*"

"Better never than on the rebound."

That's when Richard should have turned and run. Back to New York, back to London, or straight to the closest beach to throw himself in and start swimming for Tahiti. He knew he should, but he couldn't. All he could do was stand there listening, a cold, sick dread trickling down his spine.

"Don't be a fool, Susan. You've been in love with him since you were twelve years old."

"You're forgetting one very important thing, Meredith."

"What's that?"

"Richard doesn't love me."

Hell no, he didn't. Still, Richard felt like he'd been kicked, punched, slapped and doused with cold water.

The heart and arrow carved around his initials on the old mahogany desk burned like a brand in his memory. So did Susan sliding the folder over it, the sparkle dying in her eyes when he asked her if she'd seen Dr. Cade, the softness of her mouth and the way she'd yielded to him under the Christmas tree.

Of course she loved him. A blind man could see it. Even he could, now.

"You can read his mind," Meredith said. "Can't you make him love you?"

This was one shock too many, the third nasty curve he'd been thrown in a horse barn in less than a week. Richard felt numb, dazed, his brain short-circuiting on overload.

"I can*not* read his mind," Susan retorted. "How many times do I have to tell you I just get feelings from him sometimes. That's all."

It was enough, finally, to send Richard spinning around and out of the barn. The balloon in his chest was about to explode. He took the edge off it by lighting a cigarette, sucked smoke into his lungs and wished—hell—he didn't know what he wished. His father said wishing wouldn't make it so, that you could wish in one hand, spit in the other and see which one filled up faster. A real smartass, his father.

Grinding the cigarette under his heel, Richard broke into a run. He ran away from the house, away from Susan and her gift, and the spirit hovering behind him, but mostly he ran from himself. When a fence got in his way he vaulted it, all except the last one he came to, which he had to climb because it was two rails higher than the others. He ran out of wind in the middle of the paddock it enclosed and stopped to catch his breath.

A half-dozen yearlings grazing in the stretch of pasture beyond raised their heads and looked at him. Richard felt a twinge at the base of his skull, took it for a muscle spasm, tried to rub it away but couldn't. Nor could he swallow the lump he felt in his throat as he took in the beauty of the blue-misted hills ringing Cicada Ranch, the pristine whiteness of the barns, the sunlight gleaming on the hides of the horses.

The spirit was right. He didn't belong here. He didn't belong anywhere.

"Happy goddamned Thanksgiving," Richard muttered, wheeling around to head back to the house.

The balloon in his chest felt like a lump of lead. So did his legs. He wasn't sure he could climb the impossibly high six-rail fence again and looked around to see if there was an easier way out. He started toward the barn the paddock circled, wondering why this barn was set apart from the others, why the fence posts were set in concrete, why the corners were braced.

It came to him in an icy jolt of recollection that froze him to the spot a good thirty yards shy of the fence. He remembered Meredith sitting at the kitchen island telling him Flagmaster was alive and well—in his own private barn and reinforced paddock.

He remembered it just as Flagmaster himself stepped halfway around the far corner of the barn, swung his head toward Richard and looked him square in the eye.

14

FLAGMASTER DIDN'T LOOK like a monster. He looked like a stallion in his prime, a retired champion out for a stroll to survey his domain and soak up some rays. He stood seventeen hands high—and about twenty yards away from Richard. His ebony hide rippled with muscle, twelve hundred pounds of strength, speed and sheer goddamned meanness.

He'd never killed anybody—crippled a jockey and an exercise boy, but never killed anybody. Sportswriters had written of Flagmaster, as they'd written of Secretariat, that his closest competition was the wind.

His records in the Kentucky Derby and the Preakness still stood, which meant Richard had two chances of beating him to the fence—slim and none. His heart slammed in his throat, the sweat on his brow chilled in a lift of wind that fluttered the white-streaked tail that gave Flagmaster his name.

With a deep rumble in his chest, the stallion lowered his head and stepped clear of the barn. The muscle in Richard's neck spasmed but he didn't dare rub it, just thanked God he was downwind so Flagmaster couldn't smell the panic pumping through him, and took a sideways step toward the fence.

The stallion's nostrils flared and his ears pricked forward. Flagmaster swung himself neatly around to face Richard. Big as a boxcar and agile as a pony. Just Richard's luck. The wind shifted suddenly and Flagmaster lifted his head higher, his nostrils straining. Any second now the stallion would have his scent. Knowing he was sunk, Richard bolted for the fence.

He had no idea half a ton could move so fast. From the corner of his eye he saw Flagmaster leap after him, felt a moment's awe at his speed and power, then focused on the fence and saving his ass. He had a jump on the stallion, but not much of one, and poured every ounce of strength he had into driving his legs as fast as he could.

The fence jerked wildly up and down in front of him as Flagmaster's hoofbeats pounded closer. He wasn't going to make it. Richard knew it, had known before he broke for the fence he didn't have a prayer. But he had a choice, one last choice. He chose not to die running and scared out of his mind, and skidded to a halt. He'd spent his life scared and running and, by God, he'd had enough.

"You want me? Here I am!" he shouted, spinning toward the charging stallion and flinging his arms wide.

Startled by the sudden flash of movement in front of him, Flagmaster shied and veered to the left. He swung his head up, bugled, and rolled an eye at Richard. Blinding white light and the headache from hell exploded in Richard's head. Slivers of pain shot across his skull, a red haze flashed across his line of vision. Black spots, the ground and sky blurred together, then leaped back into focus as Richard shook his head, willed himself not to think about the pain and lunged after Flagmaster waving his arms.

"Come on!" he yelled. "Come and get me!"

The stallion spun on his rear quarters and bolted, flinging clods of turf behind him. One struck Richard like a fist in the chest. He barely felt it, just wiped dirt from his eyes and stared openmouthed at Flagmaster racing away from him with his tail lifted high.

About fifteen yards away the stallion wheeled around, his ears flicking up and down, his withers twitching. Richard laughed. It was a hysterical laugh, shaky with relief that he was still alive and Flagmaster was a bully. Scratch one, his father always said, and you found a coward. His father, Richard figured, ought to know.

The stallion snorted and raked the ground with one hoof. Richard was not impressed. Adrenaline sang in his veins, triumph swelled his chest. Sticking his thumbs in his ears, he waggled his fingers at Flagmaster and gave him the raspberry. "Get out of town, you old faker."

"He's not a faker," Susan said behind him. "You are."

Richard glanced at her over his shoulder. She stood on the third rail of the fence, her hands wrapped around the top, her nails digging into the wood.

"What's that supposed to mean?"

"It means Flagmaster isn't a bully or a coward and you're a fool if you think so. He's confused, that's all, not quite sure what to make of you."

"I think he knows what to make of me all right—lunch."

"Then why aren't you flat on your back with his hoof-print in the middle of your forehead?"

"Well obviously—" The chill that crawled up Richard's back stopped him. He remembered High Brow, Meredith's amazement that the filly took to him, the colors that spun in his head when he'd looked in her eyes, the red he'd seen just now. And the headache. The god-awful headache pulsing at the base of his skull. He had no idea what was going on here and didn't want to know.

"—because he's already eaten," he finished.

Susan smiled. Flagmaster rumbled. Richard swung his head around to look at him, caught the stallion's eye, and felt the jolt up his back all the way to his toes. A wary, distrustful orange surged inside his head. He shut his eyes, but still saw orange. Not only saw it, but felt the emotions embedded in it, knew they were coming from Flagmaster. And that Susan, goddamn her, knew it, too. He didn't know how he knew she knew, but he did.

"Get me out of here, Susan."

"I can't. No!" She flung up a hand as he started to pivot toward her. "Don't turn your back on him!"

The menacing snort from Flagmaster thrummed up Richard's spine and spun him back to face the stallion. He'd danced a dozen steps closer, but stopped when Richard looked at him, and flattened his ears against his head.

"You got yourself into this," Susan said. "You have to get yourself out."

"If I had the foggiest goddamn clue how," he replied, taking a small, surreptitious step backward, "I would."

"I wish I could tell you, but I can't. It wouldn't be—ethical."

"This is no time for scruples, Susan." Richard backed another step closer to the fence.

"You'll never make it."

"The hell I won't."

On the ball of his right foot Richard whirled and raced for the fence with Flagmaster's furious bugle ringing in his ears. Ahead of him, Susan's face swam in red mist. He focused on it and ran, ignoring the thunder of Flagmaster's hooves behind him.

The rails were too close together to slide through, which meant he'd have to go over the fence with twelve hundred pounds of maddened stallion hot on his heels. He wouldn't have time to climb it, he'd have to jump for the top rail and pray to God he made it. If he didn't—Richard blanked the thought out of his head, felt the earthshaking rumble of

Flagmaster's hooves rattle his teeth and gathered himself to make the leap.

When he launched himself at the fence, Susan stretched herself over it to catch him. Richard grasped her upper arms as she locked her hands on his elbows, caught the third rail with his right foot and pushed. Flagmaster's teeth closed on his left ankle, and denim ripped as Susan bowed her back to drag him over the top rail. Gravity yanked him out of the stallion's jaws and sent him sailing with Susan toward the ground on the opposite side of the fence.

In midair he managed to reverse their positions so he landed first, flat on his back with Susan on top of him. The impact knocked the wind out of him and shot the sky with streaking stars. He barely heard Flagmaster's frustrated bugle over the ringing in his ears, just clutched Susan to him and thanked God he was alive.

She pushed herself up and blinked at him, her breath coming hard and shallow, her pulse throbbing in the hollow of her throat. Her breasts, pushed against his chest, swelled in the gaping front of her shirt.

The fool who said redheads shouldn't wear red had never seen Susan in gray-striped red flannel. It made her hair glow, her eyes shimmer, and Richard ache to have her. He drew a breath, enough to ask, "Are you okay?"

"Yes. Are you?"

"I'll let you know when I can breathe again," Richard said, grasping her shoulders and pulling her mouth up to his.

He intended to make sure Susan Cade never drew a steady breath again. Not because she loved him or he loved her, but because he wanted to kiss her, because he wanted her. He didn't give a damn about her feelings or her father's .45. Susan not only let him, she clenched his hair in her hands and took his tongue into her mouth.

It was heaven, sweet heaven. And complete surrender. She tasted like coffee and desire, smelled like liniment and lavender. And it was wrong, wrong as hell. Because he didn't love her, because all he did was want her. What a lousy time to develop a conscience. Knowing he'd regret it for the rest of his life, Richard cupped her face and broke the kiss.

"I wish I was selfish enough to tell you I love you so you'd sleep with me, Susan, but I'm not. I'm sorry."

"Who said I—" Her eyes went wide, then she slapped his hands away from her face and pushed herself off him. "Damn you, Richard! I thought Meredith was the only snoop in the family!"

Shoving himself up with one hand, he trapped Susan's ankle in the other as she tried to scramble free of him. He was right. Even through the leather thickness of her boot his fingers spanned it with room to spare.

"I didn't mean to hear anything, Susan. I was just passing by—"

"Horseshit!" she cried, kicking free of his grasp. "That's what Meredith always says!"

Then she sprang to her feet and sprinted away from him. Richard lurched up behind her, took one running step on his right foot, then crumpled to the ground when he brought his weight down on his left. Pain sliced up his Achilles tendon and roared through his head.

Pulling up his torn pant leg, he pushed down his sock and saw Flagmaster's teeth marks on his ankle just above the scuffed heel of his white leather Nike. The skin wasn't broken, but a nasty bruise was already spreading up his calf.

Behind him, the stallion rumbled, a nasty, equine gotcha chuckle. Hobbling to his feet, he glared over his shoulder at Flagmaster standing at the fence, just barely able to get his head over the top rail.

"We'll see who gets the last laugh," Richard told him grimly, and went limping after Susan.

15

HE COULDN'T FIND SUSAN anywhere, though he searched every barn, every stall, every tack room. Twice.

She was hiding from him. He knew it, could almost see her ducking into dark corners ahead of him, darting between barns to evade him with her heart skipping in her throat.

The balloon in his chest was stretched to breaking with anger and frustration; at himself for being so blind and thickheaded, at Susan for being so vindictive. If she'd intended to get even with him for not recognizing her by throwing him to Flagmaster, she'd succeeded.

When his ankle gave out Richard gave up, hobbled outside into the sunshine beyond the shadow of the foaling barn, drew a lungful of air and bellowed, "Susan! Susan!"

"Hold it down, Rich," Loren Cade answered. "You're scarin' the hosses."

Richard turned around and saw Susan's father, his Stetson pushed back on his head, ambling toward him from the next nearest barn with a battered metal bucket in one hand, a pitchfork in the other. The dream he'd had of Susan in the car the day before—or was it a scrambled premonition?—flashed through Richard's head.

"You might want to get your .45, Loren."

"Why's that, son?"

"I'm not sure, but I think I may be going plum crazy."

Think, hell. He knew he was. It was the only logical explanation. Sane people didn't see colors with their eyes shut, didn't sense emotions in them. Especially from a horse.

"That so." Loren put down the bucket, stuck the fork in the ground and wrapped his fingers around the handle. "You do look a mite ruffled."

"Unraveled," Richard corrected him. Like a frayed piece of rope. Or a man who wasn't wrapped too tight to begin with. "I'd take it as a kindness if you'd put me out of my misery."

And Susan's, he thought, before I hurt her again.

"Who you been wrestlin'?" Loren gave his dirty sweater and torn pant leg a sharp-eyed once-over. "Anybody I know?"

"Flagmaster," Richard said. He'd had a moment's weakness, not a death wish, which meant he hadn't completely lost his mind. Not yet, anyway.

"Guess we know who won."

"Have you seen Susan?"

"Nope." Loren shook his head, his gaze sliding away from Richard. "Not since breakfast."

"Meredith?"

Loren looked back at him. "B'lieve she went back to the house to give Consuella a hand with the cookin'."

"Maybe Susan went with her?"

"Couldn't say." Loren's gaze slipped away again as he turned his head and scratched his neck.

You're lying, Richard wanted to tell him, but didn't. It was never a good idea to argue with a man holding a pitchfork, especially one who'd already threatened to shoot you. He wasn't that crazy. Not yet. But he could feel it hanging out there just off the metaphoric horizon, waiting for the right moment to swoop down on him.

"If you see Susan, tell her I'm looking for her, would you?" Richard turned away, then abruptly back. "She already knows, but tell her anyway."

"Sure thing." Loren pushed his Stetson farther back and scratched his head.

Richard smiled and limped toward the house, savoring the image of Loren standing flat-footed in a brown cloud of—*Hold it*. He stopped. *A brown cloud of puzzlement*. That's what he'd thought—that's what he'd *seen*. How in hell—*why* in hell was he seeing all this weird stuff inside his head? He couldn't remember the last time he'd cleaned his contacts. Maybe that was it. Please God, that was it.

He found Meredith in the kitchen, basting the turkey in its blue enamel roaster on top of the stove. Consuella stood at the sink humming and washing lettuce. The windows were fogged, the air warm and spicy.

Richard's throat clenched. He was crazy all right. Crazy to believe he could make a place for himself here. Out of his head to think he could survive the holidays in the bosom of his family.

His resolve to stop running and stop being scared evaporated like the steam rolling off the potatoes boiling on the stove. He was scared, all right, scared out of his mind by what had happened in Flagmaster's paddock and just now with Loren, certain that if he stayed he'd hurt Susan again. He wouldn't mean to, but he would.

Almost as much as he wanted her, he wanted to run. But if he did, he'd be running from himself, from whatever was happening to him, and that scared him more than anything. Susan knew what it was, she'd confessed as much. Ethical or not, he had to find a way to make her tell him. And a way to stop hurting her. He couldn't do either one if he ran.

Meredith looked up at him then, her face pink with heat, a squeeze tube full of turkey juice in her hand. "What happened to you?"

"I met Flagmaster," he said shortly. "But before that I overheard you and Susan talking in the foaling barn."

That's all he said, but that's all he had to say.

Meredith blanched. A drop of juice dripped from the tube. Consuella stopped humming, dropped the lettuce in the sink and scurried out of the room.

"You had no right to listen to a private conversation."

"That never stopped *you*. And right or wrong I heard."

"Let me guess." Meredith dropped the basting tube in the pan and jammed her hands on her hips. "In typical Richard fashion, you're leaving."

"No, not this time. I'm staying."

Meredith blinked at him. "Did Flagmaster kick you in the head?"

"No, bit my ankle. I'm staying because I need Susan."

A slow, jubilant smile spread across Meredith's face.

"You're in love with her."

"No."

"But you just said—"

"No, Meredith, *you* said. I want Susan. I want her with every fiber of my being, but I am not in love with her. Which I just told her."

For an instant her blue eyes blazed, and he thought she'd slap him. Instead Meredith snatched the basting tube out of the roaster, gave it a vicious squeeze and hosed him with turkey juice. It dripped fragrantly down his sweater, soaked into his jeans and splashed the toes of his Nikes.

Fortunately it had been in the tube long enough to cool off, and because he figured it was the least he deserved, Richard only grimaced and asked, "Feel better?"

"How *could* you!" Meredith screeched at him. "What a stinking mean thing to do!"

"That's exactly why I told her. With any luck she'll hate me now."

"This is the most rotten, selfish thing you've ever done, Richard!"

"No, it's the third," he confessed. Hell, why not? Make the break a clean one, no matter how deeply it cut. "The first most rotten, selfish thing I ever did was piss away my trust fund on Alfreda and land on my grandmother's doorstep dead-ass broke. The second was grabbing the plane ticket you offered so I could cozy up to Susan, take her to the track and recoup my losses."

Meredith blinked, stunned, then breathed shakily, "You bastard."

"Exactly."

"You can't forget, can you? You still hate Susan because she broke your nose."

"No, Meredith. I don't hate Susan. If I did I'd just take her and be done with her."

Brushing half-congealed turkey fat off the front of his sweater, Richard turned to go change, caught a flash of red in the mudroom doorway from the corner of his eye and spun around abruptly. Susan stood there, her eyes huge, her face the same bleached, dead white as the turkey.

He had no idea how much she'd heard, but it didn't matter. He'd done it again, God help him. He'd hurt her.

"Susan." Richard spread his hands and took a step toward her. "Please, I—"

"You son of a bitch," she said, then doubled her right fist and punched him in the nose.

For the second time that day Richard saw stars, but only for a second. They winked out in a red haze flashed with black. He didn't feel any pain, only a sickening crunch followed by an ear-ringing numbness that he knew from experience would blossom soon enough into genuine hurt.

The pain was in the colors streaming behind Susan as she whirled away from him—red anger and black devastation—swirling in a jet trail of amethyst so deep and dark it was almost indigo. The emotions hit him like a fist—in the gut, not the nose—and staggered him as Susan slammed out of the house.

"She hates you," Meredith said. "No doubt about it."

"Not any more than I do." Richard blinked owlishly, trying to figure out why all of a sudden the weird stuff he was seeing was blurred. "Dammit. I lost a lens."

"Before or after you lost your mind?"

"Stuff it, step-brat. Help me find it." Richard dropped to his knees and started feeling around on the floor. "While we're at it, help me think of a way to make this up to Susan."

"I like crucifixion myself," she said, joining him on all fours. "Or maybe castration."

"You helped get me into this, Meredith." Richard clamped a hand around her wrist. "You're going to help get me out."

"The hell I did." She tried, but couldn't wrench free. "The hell I will."

"You connived to get me out here and don't bother denying it. You connived to get Susan to London last spring, too. I figured out that much from what I overheard."

"So what if I did? Why should I help you?"

"Because if you don't, Lumpy's going to get an earful about your plans for High Brow."

"It's Luke." Meredith glared at him. "And that's blackmail."

"I know. Neat, isn't it?"

"You really are a rotten, selfish person."

"A product of my upbringing," Richard told her grimly. "Now connive, Meredith. I've got enough on my conscience without Susan Cade's broken heart."

16

HER HEART WASN'T BROKEN, not completely, anyway, since she'd known since she was twelve that Richard didn't love her—but Susan wasn't at all sure about her knuckles.

It was hard to tell because her fingers were swollen and already faintly bruised, but they didn't feel broken. She had a few other aches and twinges from the fall, and a sore nose, which was her own silly fault. Only a stupid empath, or one incensed beyond reason, went around punching people.

But it was worth it. For fifteen whole seconds she hadn't wished she was dead or that she'd stayed in the barn hiding. She'd been about to give it up as ridiculously juvenile behavior when her father told her Richard was looking for her and *knew* that she knew it.

Misreading the message as a sign that he'd realized his gift, she'd raced up to the house and through the mud-room just in time to hear him confess his motives for coming to Cicada Ranch. It served her right, Susan supposed, for all the times she'd told Meredith eavesdroppers always overheard what they were meant, for their own good, never to know.

At least he'd be leaving. Susan knew he would, because Richard always did. When the going got tough, he got going. Thank God for that, she thought, pacing her bedroom with an ice bag pressed to her knuckles. She'd never be able to put her heart and her pride back together under his nose. It would be hard enough in front of Meredith and

Luke. Not to mention her father, Rufus and Consuella—everyone who either knew or guessed that she loved him. Always had, and always would.

That was the hell of it. No matter how angry she was, how hurt and used she felt, she loved him. What a fool, what a turkey. Consuella should've stuffed and roasted her for dinner. Which, Susan realized, as her gaze fell on the clock on her bedside table, she was going to miss if she didn't get into the shower in the next five minutes.

Meredith the Mouth would explain, whether Susan wanted her to or not, so no one would expect her to join them. But she needed the comfort of her family, people who loved her for who she was, not what. Besides, unbelievably, she was hungry, and when Consuella said dinner at three, she meant on the dot, on the stroke.

Which is what Susan nearly had when she walked down the hall a half hour later in a long-sleeve lavender knit dress, with pearl buttons at her throat and clipped to her ears, waved to her father sitting stiffly in a suit in the living room with Luke and Rufus, glanced through the kitchen archway and saw Richard at the island carving the turkey. He wore a double-breasted navy suit, lavender shirt, patterned tie and his glasses. Not the black horn-rims she remembered, but very chic, very slim tortoise-shell frames.

Either he saw her in the doorway or sensed the fresh wave of anger and humiliation that swept through her, for he looked up. His nose was twice its normal size, which made Susan's twinge sympathetically.

"Happy Turkey Day, Susan." He smiled and held up the wishbone. A few scraps of meat still clung to it. "Want to flip me for it?"

At Foxglove, she and Richard had always flipped for the wishbone, and Richard had always won. He'd always used a two-headed coin, until Bea caught him at it. Susan wanted to flip him, all right—flat onto his back. Instead she stalked into the dining room where Meredith, dressed in blue lace-trimmed wool, was lighting candles on the table.

"What's he doing here?" she demanded in a low voice.

"What's who doing here?"

"Richard," Susan said between clenched teeth.

Meredith blew out the match and looked at her. "I invited him to my wedding. Remember?"

"But I thought—" No, she'd assumed. This was an unexpected turn, behavior totally out of character for Richard. "Never mind."

Small wonder Susan's appetite vanished. She wished she could vanish with it, back to her room, the stables, anywhere. Her insides were shaking and so were her hands. How could she sit at a table with Richard after the way she'd kissed him?

"Make way for the bird," he said behind her.

Gripping a chair for support, Susan glanced at him coming through the archway bearing the sliced turkey on a Wedgwood platter. Except for his puffy nose and a slight limp, he looked as cool and urbane as he always did, while she was a mess of hot, sticky emotions.

Until she remembered how gallantly, and how arrogantly and condescendingly, he'd rubbed her nose in her feelings. Then her temper flared, her shoulders squared and her chin came up. What did she see in this jerk? What had she ever seen in him?

While he'd cleaned up for dinner and put ice on his nose, Richard had asked himself the same question. He'd wondered, too, if she'd hate him now, and got his answer looking at her. He didn't see colors or feelings, but he didn't need to—the ugh-what-a-slug expression on her face said it all.

It was a lovely heart-shaped face, and pale because of him. He regretted that, more than he thought he would, and resolved to put the color back in her cheeks. He might as well have resolved to climb Mount Everest on his hands and knees, for crawl was clearly what Susan intended to make him do. She sat across from him during dinner, as remote and cold as a mountain, impervious to his attempts to catch her eye with a smile.

The first time she lifted her wineglass with her right hand, the mouthful of oyster stuffing he'd just swallowed stuck in his throat. Her knuckles were a swollen, sick shade of yellow green, and Richard realized that until now she'd been careful to pick up her glass with her left.

But she was distracted, her head turned to talk to Rufus, and didn't notice Lumpy gazing at her hand. Richard did, but with his mouth full all he could do was grab his water goblet and swallow as fast as he could without choking.

"Hey, Suz." Luke caught her hand as she put down her glass. "Is there a connection between your black-and-blue knuckles and old Four Eyes' puffy nose or do I just have an overactive imagination?"

He gave Richard a look that said there'd better not be. So did Loren Cade. Meredith shot him one that said run for your life, but Richard stayed put, laid his fork on his plate and waited for Susan's reply.

"Yes, there is." She lifted her hand out of Luke's and tucked it in her lap. "We had a run-in with Flagmaster."

"*You* had a run-in with Flagmaster?" Luke's sandy brows shot up. "I thought the old monster ate out of your hand."

"He was upset," Susan replied with a shrug. "He doesn't like strangers in his paddock. I got banged up a little rescuing Richard and so did he."

It wasn't exactly a rescue as Richard recalled it, but he didn't argue. He couldn't believe Susan had lied, didn't understand why she hadn't told Lumpy and Loren the truth, the whole rotten, stinking, selfish truth.

"Not much of a horseman, are you?" Luke said to him.

"I never claimed to be," Richard replied.

"Lemme guess," Luke went on. "You were wearing your contacts and didn't recognize Flagmaster, right?"

"Luke," Meredith said, a thread of warning in her voice.

"He's the one who claims to have twenty-twenty vision, cutie. Not me."

Across the table from Richard, Susan held her breath. Richard leaned back in his chair and bent his right elbow on the arm. Her chest suddenly felt tight, as though there was somebody in there blowing up a balloon. When Richard reached for his wineglass with his left hand, Susan realized he'd hardly touched it. His fingers closed on the stem, then opened. The signet ring on his pinkie flashed in the candlelight. So did his eyes.

"Even with my glasses," he said evenly, "I can recognize a jackass."

"Good one, Rich." Loren gave a hoot of laughter and slapped his hand on the table. "Gotcha there, Luke!"

Richard smiled. Luke turned red above his shirt collar. When the phone rang in the kitchen, Consuella got up to answer it, but Meredith waved her back into her chair.

"Luke and I will get it," she said, hooking his elbow and pulling him to his feet as she passed behind him.

"Sometimes that boy just don't know when t'quit," Loren said, passing the mashed potatoes to Richard.

"He never did," Richard agreed, turning his head toward Susan.

He caught her smiling, but not at him. The quick duck of her chin told him so. She'd lie for him, but she wouldn't look at him. Richard swallowed his irritation with a sip of water. He could be patient, he thought, so long as the weird stuff stayed away.

He thought he could eat two pieces of pumpkin pie, too, but had to quit or explode midway through the second. Rufus was on his third, Consuella clearing dishes around him. Loren and Lumpy and Susan had carried theirs into the living room to watch football on the big-screen TV. Richard pushed his pie away and got up to join them.

"Pssst!"

He glanced over his left shoulder and saw Meredith leaning around the archway crooking her finger at him. As he walked toward her, she backed into the kitchen.

"Don't even ask," he said in a low, firm voice, "because I won't do it. I will not apologize to Lumpy again."

"Luke," she reminded him. "Your grandmother called, Richard. She asked if you were here. I lied and told her you'd sent me a postcard from Cancun. Then I called Mother. She gave Mrs. Barton-Forbes our number, but told her she hadn't seen or talked to you. She and Daddy got home late last night and Mrs. Clark hadn't had time to fill her in, so I did."

The balloon in Richard's chest tightened. "Why Cancun?"

"She sounded worried and I felt sorry for her. Cancun was the first place I thought of."

Worried, my foot, Richard thought darkly, hooking a finger in his tie to loosen it before the balloon strangled him. A sudden swell of crowd roar from the TV and a whoop from Loren drew his attention to the living room.

He saw a running back dancing in a snow-banked end zone and Susan, loosening the top two buttons of her dress and rubbing her throat. Just like he was, Richard realized with a start, as he dropped his hand and looked back at Meredith.

"Did she say anything about my mother?"

"No." Meredith pursed her lips, thinking. "She mentioned Devlin, but not your mother."

Richard's overfull stomach knotted. "What about Devlin?"

"She said, 'That old fart has lied to me for the last time.' Then she hung up, didn't even say goodbye." Meredith shook her head, her mouth puckered. "And I felt sorry for the old bat."

Richard felt sorry for Devlin. If anyone could handle his grandmother he supposed it was Devlin, since he had damn near forty years experience. But he was old and frail now, and half-blind. Eerie, Richard thought. Just this morning he'd been worrying about Devlin. Was it another premonition or his guilty conscience? Which kicked into overdrive as Susan came through the archway behind him carrying a stack of dessert plates.

He caught a glimpse of her from the corner of his eye and turned his head slightly to look at her. She walked past him as if he weren't even there, her scent the same color as her dress and his shirt and the rainbow spanning her shoulders.

Oh no. Not again. Lifting his glasses with one hand, Richard wiped the other over his eyes and blinked at Susan. She was looking at him over her left shoulder, but turned abruptly back to the sink, turned on the water and started rinsing the plates. The lavender arc was gone and so was Meredith.

Drawing a deep breath, Richard walked around the island and leaned against it. Susan's head was bent, her hair falling forward. He wanted to slip his arms around her and kiss the nape of her neck, until he remembered Susan telling Meredith she could sometimes sense his feelings. With an effort, he pushed the thought out of his head, and braced the heels of his hands on the countertop. "I didn't want or intend you to hear what I said to Meredith, Susan."

"I'm sure you didn't," she snapped, shutting off the water and stacking the plates on the drain board.

"I'm sorry, Susan. I've never been this sorry for anything in my life."

"You didn't have to lie." She spun around to face him, hurt, angry tears glittering in her eyes. "Or try to seduce me. I would have gone to the track with you, Richard. All you had to do was ask me."

"You know why I didn't. And you know that it's as much your fault as it is mine."

"Oh *really*?" Susan thrust her weight on one hip and locked her arms together at her waist. "How do you figure that?"

"You've had a chip on your shoulder since I got here, just because I didn't recognize you," Richard retorted, angry himself now, but keeping his voice low. "How the hell was I supposed to, Susan? I hadn't seen you in eight years for God's sake. Your hair's a different color. If you'd been wearing a name tag, maybe—"

"All right," she cut in. "I get your point."

"If it makes you feel any better, trying to seduce you had nothing to do with my plan to take you to the track."

"It doesn't."

"Then why don't you prance into the living room and tell your Daddy why I really came? I'm sure he'd be pleased as punch to knock my head off."

Susan's chin shot up defiantly. "If I thought as little of me as you obviously do, I would. In a heartbeat."

"You're wrong, Susan. I think a lot of you." Richard pushed himself off the island and a step closer to her. "You're all I've been able to think about since I got here."

"Oh please," she said disgustedly, and tried to push past him. Richard caught her elbow. "You know I do, Susan. Just like you know what happened to me in Flagmaster's paddock."

"Let me go." Susan's voice shook from the intensity of their anger—and their desire for each other, singing back and forth between them where his hand touched her.

"Not until you tell me what happened, Susan. You said all I had to do was ask."

"Not about this. I can't help you."

"You mean you won't. Why? Still trying to get even?"

"If I'd wanted to get even I would've broken your nose *again*." Her eyes flashing, Susan jerked her elbow out of his hand. "And if you don't stay away from me, Richard, the next time I *will*."

17

APPARENTLY RICHARD thought Susan meant it, and she did—for five whole seconds, all the time it took her to break the connection between them, stalk into the living room and realize she was behaving like a child. Or Wonder Woman with PMS.

She knew Richard didn't love her, so why was she acting like this? Why did she feel as though part of her had been cut out? If she could just figure it out, Susan thought, rubbing her tingling elbow, maybe she could stop feeling so empty.

She expected, or maybe she just hoped that Richard would follow her, but he didn't. When Susan turned around and walked past the archway toward her office, he stayed in the kitchen to help Meredith and Consuella with the dishes.

She should've been relieved, but she wasn't, and wouldn't be, she told herself, until Richard drove away in the rented Tempo.

But when he did on Friday afternoon, just as Susan was leaving the foaling barn with Loren after checking on Peggity, her heart turned to ice as she watched the red Ford wind its way up the drive. Until Loren laid his hands on her shoulders and told her Richard was returning the car and that Meredith, who'd spent the day in Santa Barbara meeting with clients, would pick him up.

That's when Susan knew she was in big trouble.

Whether or not Richard acknowledged his gift consciously, it was still operational subconsciously. The yellow rose and the thought he'd plucked out of her head under the Christmas tree proved that. So did the lavender shirt he'd worn on Thanksgiving. Coincidence, some would say, but Susan knew better. If she wasn't extremely careful she'd betray her feelings, and if Richard picked up on them, if he touched her again, no matter how innocently or accidentally, she'd give him anything he wanted, and everything she'd ever dreamed of.

The sound of hoofbeats jerked Susan out of her thoughts. Banner, Flagmaster's black two-year-old son, came pounding around the last turn of the half-mile exercise track it had cost Susan a year's salary to build. He was running easily with Paulie O'Gilbert hunched over his withers, the white-streaked tail like his sire's streaming behind him. Susan pressed the stem of the stopwatch in her hand as the colt shot past the furlong pole in front of her and Paulie rose in his stirrups.

Twenty-one seconds flat in the quarter. An incredible, phenomenal time. A burst of joy and excitement shot through Susan, the first she'd felt since Thursday afternoon. Beautiful little speed demon that she was, High Brow would be hard pressed to beat Banner.

She could see it now: the winner's circle at Churchill Downs, Banner standing serene and victorious, a horseshoe of red roses draped over his sweat-darkened withers and Angel Cordero or Chris McClaren on his back; his trainer, Loren Cade, grinning on one side of him, and she, the proud owner on the other, one hand on Banner's flank, the other held tightly by —

The image shattered inside Susan's head. She'd forgotten her Kentucky Derby Fantasy was one of her Richard Fantasies. Now that she thought about it, Susan realized

all of her fantasies were Richard Fantasies. He was the one
constant in all her dreams. That's why she felt so empty
and bereft. Not because she'd lost Richard—you can't lose
something you've never had—but because she'd lost her
dreams.

Her excitement faded along with her joy, and she sensed
that she was being watched. Slapping the stopwatch
against her chest, Susan spun around and caught Luke
trying to peek at Banner's time over her shoulder.

"Little early in the day for you to be out spying on the
competition, isn't it?"

"Who me?" Luke pressed a hand innocently to his chest.
"What competition?"

"Ha ha, Hardin." Susan slipped the stopwatch into her
pocket. "You're worried or you wouldn't be here."

"Horse puckey. I'm here to partake of Consuella's world-
famous Saturday-morning Mexican brunch."

Susan glanced at her wristwatch. "At eight-thirty?
Consuella doesn't serve brunch until eleven."

"I don't want Four Eyes beating me to the scrambled-
egg-and-chile enchiladas."

"Richard," Susan corrected him, turning back to the
track as Banner came prancing up to the rail.

Except for his disposition, the colt was a carbon copy
of Flagmaster. He'd inherited his calm-as-lake-water-on-
a-still-day temperament from his dam, Peggity, a fine stake
mare until she'd strained the tendons in the leg and developed the swollen fetlock plaguing her in this pregnancy.
Her last, Susan swore, feeling a tug of worry for the mare.
Peggity had given her Banner and three other Flagmaster
colts. The foal she carried now would make five of her
bloodline. That was enough.

"Some run, huh, boss?" Paulie grinned at Luke, loosened the chin strap of his helmet and swung his leg over

Banner's withers to dismount as Susan caught the colt's headstall.

The boy's flushed face shone with excitement. Susan's hand tingled with the thrill of the run, telegraphed to her on the colt's pulsating, electric-blue essence as she stripped off his bridle and replaced it with a soft hackamore clipped to a lead.

"Not bad," Luke said grudgingly. "Guess the doc here was right. Maybe you do have the makings of a jockey."

"Told you." Paulie dropped nimbly to the ground, still grinning over his shoulder as he loosened Banner's girth. "Gonna let me ride for you now?"

"If you can beat High Brow on this spindly-legged ink pot, we'll talk."

Banner flicked one ear back and turned his head toward Luke. "It's a joke," Susan whispered to him, tugging his blanket off the rail as she ducked beneath it. Banner gave a snort, swung his head away and stamped a hoof.

Paulie dragged his saddle off Banner, flung it over the rail and held out his gloved right hand to Luke. "Betcha fifty bucks High Brow eats our dust."

"Never bet what you can't afford to lose," Luke warned.

Wasn't that the truth, Susan thought, as she tossed Banner's blanket over his steaming back. She'd not only bet her heart, she'd bet her dreams on Richard. And lost.

Luke caught her eye as she ducked beneath Banner's chin to fasten the blanket straps. "Gimme a clue here, Suz."

"Not a chance, Hardin," she said with a smug smile.

"Okay, kid. You're on." His voice grim, but with a twinkle in his eye, Luke took Paulie's hand. "Just remember you're on loan to Dr. Cade. Don't forget who signs your paychecks."

"Maybe she'll gimme a job." Paulie grinned at Susan. "And a raise."

Not Cordero or McClaren, she decided, but O'Gilbert—Paulie O'Gilbert, his face streaked with race grime, his spiked orange hair stiff with sweat above the neon-green-and-electric-blue silks of the P. H. Cade racing stable, a red rose clamped between his teeth. So that's how you put the pieces of your heart back together, Susan thought. When a dream dies you build another one.

"Cool him out good, Paulie," she said, giving Banner an affectionate slap on the neck.

"You bet, Doc." Paulie slid Luke a wicked grin and took off his helmet as he led Banner away. "This fella's my ticket to the top."

And mine too, Susan thought, watching the colt nibble at Paulie's spiked hair. First the Derby, then the Preakness and the Belmont, for the Triple Crown and all the marbles. She smiled when Paulie gave Banner a playful cuff and the colt tossed his head. It was a good choice, an unbeatable combination, electric blue and gutsy, feisty orange.

"You sure about putting Paulie up on Banner for the race?" Luke scooped the saddle off the rail, and they started toward the barns.

"I've never been more sure of anything."

"You getting one of your hunches here, Suz?"

Susan slid him a sideways smile. "Maybe."

"Sometimes I envy you, sometimes I don't." Luke braced the lightweight racing saddle against his hip. "Like when deadbeats turn up out of nowhere to take advantage of you."

"I'm going to choke Meredith," Susan said between clenched teeth, quickly turning her head away so Luke wouldn't see the humiliated flush shooting up her throat.

"I'd be glad to finish breaking his nose for you, Suz. Just say the word."

"This time I *am* going to choke her." Susan's strides lengthened angrily. "I should've a long time ago."

"I think you're mad at the wrong person, Suz. You oughta be mad at Four Eyes."

"Richard," Susan snapped. "I am mad at him. I slugged him, didn't I?"

"Not hard enough." Luke shifted the saddle higher on his hip and hurried to keep up with her. "You're gonna do it, aren't you? You're gonna drive up to L.A. tomorrow, hit Santa Anita and make old Four Eyes his fortune back."

Susan missed a step, swung around to face Luke and jammed her hands on her hips. "Snooping in my office again, is she?"

"No, Consuella was. She saw the brochures and the map and asked Meredith when you were going. Meredith put it together from there."

"Mind your own business, Hardin." Susan stabbed her index finger in his chest. "And tell Meredith to mind hers."

"Susan." Luke caught her elbow as she spun away from him, his voice gentle. "It won't make him love you."

"I know that." She stared hard at the barns just a few yards ahead and tried not to cry. "That's not why I'm doing it. I'm doing it so he'll go away."

"Oh," Luke said, then again, brightly, "Oh. Well all right, Suz. For a minute there I thought you might still be in love with the jerk."

Not for a minute, Susan thought. For the rest of her life, God help her.

"I'll go with you. I'll even drive." Luke gave the saddle a last hike up his hip as they started toward the barns again. "It'll be worth it not to have him at the wedding."

Once Susan cleaned and stowed the tack and checked on Banner, she made for the foaling barn and Peggity's stall, with Luke tagging along behind her. He watched her examine the swollen rear fetlock, run her hands expertly along the mare's bulging flanks. Peggity stood quietly with her weight off the troublesome hoof.

"If that fetlock gets any worse," he said quietly, "it could give her trouble when she foals."

"I know." Susan stroked Peggity's muzzle, leaned her forehead between the mare's eyes, closed hers and felt the warm, golden glow that was Peggity. She sensed, too, a faint, pale shade she couldn't quite get a fix on, and frowned. "Don't worry, Peggity," she murmured to the mare. "I'll know when it's your time and I'll be here."

"You've drained the fluid, I'm sure," Luke said to her as she left the stall.

"Every time I turn around. I've iced it and rubbed it," Susan sighed worriedly. "I've tried everything but voodoo."

They were halfway to the house when they heard the scream that sounded like someone inside was strangling a chicken. "Oh no," Susan groaned, breaking into a run. "Now what?"

It was raining napkins in the kitchen. Ivory cocktail napkins with fluted, gold-stamped edges. Meredith was grabbing and flinging them by the handfuls out of a cardboard box on the island. Richard was trying to catch her wrists. Consuella stood by the sink with her apron over her face.

"Uh-oh," Luke said, plucking a crumpled napkin out of the air and handing it to Susan.

The gold-foil stamp in one corner read Lake and Meredith.

"Oh no," she gasped, clapping a hand over her mouth.

"Don't you *dare* laugh!" Meredith wheeled away from the box and pointed her index finger at Susan.

Behind her, Richard spread his hands on the island and blew the hair falling over his forehead out of his eyes. The corners of his mouth were twitching.

"Well, Meredith," Susan said, "at least they're ivory."

"Calm down, cutie." Luke walked to Meredith and laid his hands on her shoulders. "We'll just have the napkins reprinted."

"What's this *we?*" she demanded, brushing his hands away. "You haven't lifted a finger to help me with this wedding!"

"I've got a job, honey."

"What have I got? A *hobby?*" Meredith shrieked, slugging him in the solar plexus. "I don't have time to argue with the stationer and the florist and the caterer—"

"What about Four Eyes?" Luke interrupted, glaring at Richard and rubbing his ribs. "No job, lots of time on his hands. 'Course he's got no money, either. The way I hear it, that's why he came—to mooch off his relatives."

"Just *stop it*, Luke!" Meredith aimed another punch at him that he caught in his hand. Susan winced as Richard shot straight off the island, his fists doubled. "I'm sick to death of you picking on Richard! You're so jealous of him you can't see straight!"

This was a revelation, to Richard, as well as Susan. She saw it in the leap of his eyebrows above his glasses, saw the certainty of it in the ruddy flush splotching Luke's throat. Though of course he denied it, with a derisive snort.

"Me? Jealous of Four Eyes? That'll be the day!"

"You always have been!" Meredith yanked her hand out of his. "Why don't you just admit it and stop behaving like a spoiled, whiny little brat!"

"Spoiled!" Luke's eyes and the veins in his neck bulged. "Whiny!"

"*He* doesn't have a job," she shot back, her voice a petulant singsong. "*He* says he has twenty-twenty vision, not *me*. Thirty-two-inch waist, Four Eyes." Meredith jammed her hands on her hips. "And an IQ to match!"

"All right—" Susan said firmly, stepping forward to break up the argument.

"—that's enough," Richard said, finishing the thought for her as he came around the island.

They blinked at each other, stunned.

"This is *your* fault, Four Eyes."

A fraction of a second before Luke launched his right fist at Richard, Susan shouted, "Duck!" She hadn't seen the punch coming, she'd *sensed* it was coming.

Richard must have, too, for there was hardly time for him to react to her warning before Luke's fist was shooting toward his face. Still, he managed to sidestep it, push Meredith out of the way, grasp handfuls of Luke's shirtfront—and freeze at the loud metallic click of a gun being cocked.

"Hold it right there, boys," Susan's father said, calmly but firmly from the doorway behind her.

18

LOREN CADE held a steady bead on them with a shotgun, not a .45. Its long double muzzle was well oiled and gleaming, capable of blowing him and Lumpy to hell and back with only one barrel.

Behind Loren, Rufus Page held the .45, a pearl-handled Colt. Its twin was tucked in the waistband of his trousers. Cowboy guns, collector's items, or Richard, the son of a National Rifle Association member, missed his guess.

Not for a minute did Richard think Loren or Rufus would shoot them. Still, he let go of Lumpy's shirt and stepped back. Consuella peeled a corner of her apron away from her eyes, saw the guns and went screaming out of the kitchen crossing herself.

"Dad," Susan said, "this isn't necessary."

"Never you mind, Susie." Neither the barrel of the shotgun nor Loren's grip on it wavered. "Reckon it's time Luke and Richard settled this once and for all. Rufus."

He stepped around Loren, tugging the other Colt out of his trousers. Uh-oh, Richard thought, sensing where this was headed. He didn't like it, not one little bit, but took the pistol Rufus solemnly offered him, lowered his eyes, made sure the safety was on, eased the chamber open, then closed it with a sigh of relief.

Lumpy didn't bother to look, just turned pale when Rufus handed him the other pistol. So did Meredith, as she whirled toward Loren, her pulse beating visibly in her throat.

"This isn't Oplahoma, Uncle Loren."

Great, mock the man with the shotgun, Richard thought, even if it is as empty as the pistols. Frightened as she was, Meredith probably didn't realize her slip of the tongue, but Susan did. From the corner of his eye, Richard saw her press her lips tightly together.

"It was just an argument," Meredith insisted. "Nothing to get this upset about."

"That why I heard screamin' clear down to the pasture? Man can't even fix a fence 'round here these days without fisticuffs breakin' out ever' five minutes." He took a step back and gestured toward the door with the shotgun. "Let's go, boys. Take it outside where it belongs."

"This is ridiculous." Luke put the pistol down on the island. "I'm not going anywhere."

"That so?" Loren drew back the hammer on the second barrel with a solid click.

"The shotgun isn't loaded, you idiot," Richard muttered to him, "neither are the pistols. Pick it up and move."

Luke shot him a dark look, but grabbed up the Colt. Feeling Susan's eyes on him, Richard trailed him out of the kitchen.

Loren paused halfway through the door and nodded to Rufus. "Mind the womenfolk," he said gravely, then disappeared behind Richard and Luke.

Meredith made a beeline to follow them, but Susan caught her arm. "Whoa, Nellie. Let them play it out."

"Susan! They're going to shoot each other!"

"Nobody's going to shoot anybody. My father wouldn't give a loaded gun to either one of those two."

"Ohhh," Meredith said, a slow smile spreading across her face. "I get it now."

Double time, Loren marched Richard and Luke up to the front porch of the bungalow he shared with Rufus.

"That's far enough," he said, leaning the shotgun against the rail. "What'll it be, boys? Bare knuckles or gloves?"

"Your choice," Richard offered. "Or we can flip for it."

"Not on your life. I remember your two-headed quarter," Lumpy retorted. "Gloves."

"Gloves it is." Loren picked up two pairs from the porch, tossed one to each of them and took the pistols. "Me and Rufus go a round or two now and then. Helps keep us in shape."

While Loren laced Luke into his gloves, Richard took off his glasses, his shirt, shoes and socks, cuffed up his jeans, and stepped away from the porch to warm up. When he finished and opened his eyes, Loren stood waiting with his gloves. Lumpy was jumping up and down and bobbing his head from side to side.

"What's that supposed to be? Karate or something?"

"Tae kwon do," Richard replied, holding his hands out to Loren. "Korean karate."

Lumpy stopped jumping and bobbing. An oh-shit expression flickered across his face, then he smiled. "Tae kwon your own do, Four Eyes. You're still blind as a bat without your glasses."

"I don't look with my eyes." Richard tapped his right glove against his temple. "I look with my mind, with my soul. I trace the pattern of your essence—"

And he'd been doing it for the past four days, ever since he'd looked deep into High Brow's eyes. He had no idea how he knew but he did, suddenly and with perfect clarity. He knew what the lavender rainbow around Susan's shoulders was, and Loren's brown cloud of puzzlement— and the dingy, dust-covered, very old red halo circling Lumpy.

"If I were you," Luke said, smacking his gloves together. "I'd follow the pattern of my punches."

"Marquis of Queensbury rules?" Richard asked Loren, shaking off the chill the realization had given him.

"Nope. Oplahoma rules," Loren answered with a straight face and a twinkle in his eye. "Anything y'bite off y'git t'keep."

"My kind of rules," Lumpy said, squaring off on Richard.

"Hold on." Loren walked out from under the oaks shading the porch and beckoned them to follow. Once clear of the trees, Richard saw Susan and Meredith and Rufus standing on the patio watching. "This oughta do." Loren leaned against the closest oak and raised one booted foot against the trunk. "Okay, boys. Have at it."

"But they can see us," Lumpy objected.

"That's the idea, son. Women set a lotta store by this kinda thing."

With a malicious grin, Hardin whirled toward Richard and swung for the moon. Richard dodged and ducked another right. Lumpy lurched after him, but he spun deftly out of his way.

"Still a coward, huh?"

"The idea is not to get hit."

"Wrong. The idea is to punch your face in." Lumpy threw a left that missed by half a furlong.

"Want to borrow my glasses?"

"Want to borrow money?"

What did Meredith see in this clown? Richard wondered, landing a quick right jab that snapped Luke's neck and drew blood. Not much, just a trickle. The corner of Richard's mouth tingled and he tasted rust.

Weird, he thought, watching Lumpy shake his head and a lot of dust off the red wheeling around him. It was bright, vivid and very intense now. The next punch he threw barely missed.

"Hold still, goddammit!"

"How's this?" Richard dropped to the ground on his back and thumped a glove on his chest. "Have a seat, Lump."

"Smartass," Luke snarled and dived after him.

Richard rolled deftly out from under him and sprang to his feet. He was goading Lumpy and enjoying it. Whatever he had stuck in his craw—and Richard didn't for an instant think it was jealousy—it was time he unloaded it.

Breathing hard, Lumpy rolled into a sitting position, plunked his elbows on his knees and looked at Richard.

"Where the hell'd you learn this stuff?"

"The military school my father sent me to because I was such a wuss."

"Your old man's a jerk. So was mine. That's why they got along so well."

Now this made sense, a hell of a lot more than jealousy. This Richard could relate to. Remembering how clumsy and perpetually red-faced Lumpy had been, he almost felt sorry for him when he tried to get up and fell again.

"Gimme a hand, would you?"

Richard offered his right arm. Lumpy hooked his left around it, levered himself to his feet and smashed his right into Richard's jaw. Richard reeled back, stunned.

"That's for being so goddamned perfect," Lumpy said, his voice echoing in Richard's ringing ears.

Richard shook his head and straightened. He couldn't believe Hardin had sucker-punched him—or that Meredith was right.

"Whale," Loren said. "Now we're gettin' someplace."

"Obviously," Richard said, drawing a steadying breath, "you wouldn't know perfect if it bit you on the—"

"Watch it, son," Loren cautioned. "Ladies present."

Not quite present, but close enough, Richard saw, glancing at Susan and Meredith running toward them with Rufus puffing behind. With his head turned, he didn't see the right uppercut until it was almost too late. He managed to evade it, but just barely. It zipped past his ear like a bullet.

"Always got the perfect comeback, don't you?" Hardin jeered, chasing after him. "That's another reason I'm going to smash your face in."

"Cool off," Richard warned. He was having trouble checking the anger pumping through him and the impulse to punch Hardin silly. "I don't want to knock you on your can in front of Meredith."

"Good. It'll make it easier to flatten you."

He launched a flurry of punches at Richard. One glanced off Richard's chin and another off his shoulder before he managed to dance clear and fling a furious look at Loren.

"Stop this before he makes me hurt him."

"B'lieve that's what he wants you to do."

"I don't give a damn what he wants. Get me out of this," he said, realizing he'd said the same thing to Susan the day before in Flagmaster's paddock.

"No can do, son. This is your fight."

"You started it."

"Don't matter. You gotta finish it."

He should've a long time ago, Richard realized, ducking and weaving away from another hail of punches. He should've finished a lot of things. The most important one stood next to her father, with her arm around Meredith, watching him.

Richard stopped ducking. He spread his feet, lowered his arms and faced Hardin, just as he'd faced Flagmaster in his paddock. "I'm not running anymore, Lumpy. You want me, come and get me."

A predatory smile spread across Hardin's face. He raced in for the kill, his left arm drawn back, every muscle, every tendon in his arm bulging. All Richard had to do was throw up his right glove and brace himself. Lumpy plowed into it and keeled over on his back in a dazed sprawl.

The shock of the blow almost dropped Richard beside him. It reverberated up his arm, throbbed in his jaw and rang in his ears. He felt himself slipping toward the ground, saw Meredith running at a crazy uphill angle toward Lumpy. He heard the shriek she gave, and Susan's voice, like an echo inside his head, "Hold him up for me, Dad."

He managed to shake off the black spots swimming at the corners of his vision as Loren jerked him upright from behind and Susan lifted his face in her hands. He felt a jolt like the one he'd felt from High Brow as she pressed her thumbs beneath his cheekbones, splayed her fingers at the base of his skull and locked her gaze with his.

His equilibrium came flooding back; so did his hearing. He heard Lumpy groan and Rufus cackle, felt the ground settle firmly beneath his feet. He saw stars in Susan's eyes, or thought he did, little gold suns bursting in her irises, but when he blinked and shook his head again, they were gone.

"You're okay, slugger." Susan smiled, stepped away from him and dropped to one knee beside Lumpy.

What had she done to him? A second ago he'd been ready to fall on his face. *Slugger.* That's what she'd done, she'd called him slugger. Richard wanted to pound his fists on his chest and yodel like Tarzan but didn't, just watched Susan check Lumpy's pulse and peek beneath his fluttering eyelids.

"He's okay," she said. "Just dazed."

"Boy's got a jaw like glass." Loren grinned as he caught Richard's right wrist and started unlacing his glove. "Need t'work on that right, though, son. The idea ain't t'pass out next t'yer opponent."

How many times had he almost done that in self-defense class? Richard remembered falling rubber-kneed to the mat, not because he'd been hit, but because he'd hit the other guy. He would've dropped like a rock again except for Susan.

She'd done a hell of a lot more than call him slugger, he thought, and felt a chill shoot up his back. She'd known the punch had hit him as hard as it hit Lumpy and she'd done—something—to counteract it. What? he wondered, watching her help Meredith help Lumpy to his feet.

Luke was still pretty rocky and his eyes glassy, but he managed to stand on his own two feet, strip off his right glove and offer his hand to Richard. "I guess the best man won. You got a tux? I need one."

"Yeah, I've got one. But I don't think it will fit you."

"Not a tux. I need a best man. You."

Richard had never been the best anything. Not once in his whole miserable, messed-up life. He took Lumpy's hand and wished he'd knocked him on his can a long damn time ago.

"I'd be honored," he said, and meant it.

"Now our wedding will be all in the family," Meredith said, smiling as she slipped her arm through Luke's. "Susan is my maid of honor."

19

THAT NIGHT RICHARD dreamed Susan was the bride and he was the groom. She wore the killer emerald green dress and the white veil Meredith had cut to ribbons. Her father gave her away with his shotgun tucked beneath his arm.

Richard Senior and Bea were there, so was his mother, his grandmother and Alfreda. When he turned down the aisle with his bride on his arm, they fell on him like wolves. Lady Simpson, his grandmother and Alfreda tried to wrench him away from Susan; his father and Bea tried to pull him back.

They grasped and clawed until they ripped him in two. Susan ran out of the church, the white colonial church they'd attended every Sunday at Foxglove, screaming, "I can't help you! I can't help you!" Half of Richard ran after her.

High Brow stood outside, conveniently saddled. Devlin was there, too, holding a white cane and a tin cup. The sign around his neck read, "Alms for the blind and the poor." Richard jumped on the filly and raced after Susan. Loren Cade chased him on Flagmaster, his eyes as red as the stallion's, his shotgun loaded and cocked. "This is yer fight, son. Y'gotta finish it, gotta finish it, gotta finish it...."

He woke up with Loren's voice echoing inside his head, bathed in sweat, the headache pounding at the base of his skull. The clock on the nightstand said 8:20. Richard rolled slowly up on the side of the bed. His right arm still ached. He closed his eyes and rubbed it, and tried to erase the dream. The harder he tried, the more his arm hurt and the harder his head pounded.

He gave it up, leaned back against his damp pillow and let the images wash back into his mind. The pain in his arm and his head faded, but the balloon in his chest swelled with panic. He lit a cigarette and tried again to erase the dream—with the same results. The pain eased the instant he let himself sink back into the dream.

He put on his glasses and dug through the tangled sheets until he found the book he'd filched from Susan's office after she'd gone to bed. The book was hidden in a drawer of the old mahogany desk under a stack of files, and it had taken him nearly half an hour to find it with a flashlight. The title was *You Are Psychic.*

Richard reread the passages marked with a pink highlighter, the ones that had scared hell out of him in the middle of the night. They still did, but not quite as much. At least they were answers, weird and way out there in the ozone, but answers. Maybe not the right ones, maybe he should be reading *You Are Out Of Your Feeble Little Mind,* by Dr. U. R. Nuts, but at the moment this was all he had.

He paid particular attention to a section on dreams, laid the book down and tried again to wipe his dream away. The pain roared back and the dream focused this time on Devlin. When he tried to push the old manservant out of his mind, his headache erupted like a solar flare behind his closed eyelids. It backed off when he fumbled for the bedside phone and punched the number of the house in Gramercy Park.

Devlin answered on the fourth ring.

"This is Richard, Devlin. How are you?"

"Quite well, Master Richard. And you, sir?"

"No master, or sir—just Richard. Where's my grand-mother?"

"Madam is in Cancun, Mexico, trying to find you and bring you to your senses before it's too late."

It already was. Richard knew that much, anyway.

"Is she alone?"

"Your mother and your fiancée accompanied her."

"I don't have a fiancée, Devlin." *Not yet*, he added silently. "Do you have any money?"

"Do you wish to borrow some? I'd be very happy to—"

"No, but thank you. Do you have enough to buy your-self a plane ticket?"

"Yes," Devlin answered, puzzled. "Where am I going?"

"Santa Barbara. There should be a flight out of La Guardia about one this afternoon." Richard told him the name of the airline. "Can you be on it?"

"I believe I can manage that."

"Good. I'll meet you. And Devlin?"

"Yes, sir?"

"Leave my grandmother a letter of resignation."

Richard hung up, closed his eyes and felt for the head-ache. It was still there, a dull background ache, waiting to see what he'd do next. He hadn't a clue, but trusting the pain would let him know, he hid the book under his mat-tress, showered and dressed and went looking for his des-tiny.

He found a fresh pot of coffee in the kitchen and Mer-edith sitting in the great room, in a swivel chair at the oak rolltop desk by the fireplace. She was reading what looked like a prospectus.

"Where's Susan?" he asked, as he poured himself a cup of coffee.

"She and Luke drove up to L.A." Meredith bent an arm on the back of her chair and looked at him over her shoulder as he sat on the arm of the sofa by the desk. She wore reading glasses Richard had no idea she needed. "To look at some horses, they said."

"Will she mind if I have a houseguest?"

"Depends." Meredith slid her glasses down her nose and eyed him over the blue plastic frames. "Male or female?"

"Devlin. He can share the guest room with me. I'm not totally destitute. I've got a few bucks to pay for his keep, and he could be a big help to you with your wedding."

"I'd already thought of that. In fact, I'd planned to suggest it myself if you didn't."

"How did you—" Richard stopped, waiting for the headache to flare, but it didn't. "Don't tell me you can read my mind, too."

"No, just your face. You turned white as a sheet when I told you what your grandmother said." Meredith laid her glasses on the desk and swiveled the chair around to face him. "If you bring Devlin here, she'll find out and come after you. You know that, don't you?"

"Yes. I also know she'll have my mother and Alfreda with her. Devlin told me they're in Cancun trying to hunt me down and bring me to my senses."

"Too bad I didn't say Fiji." Meredith frowned and gave him a searching look. "*Have* you come to your senses, Richard?"

"I think so," he said with a smile. He'd know for sure once he saw Susan.

"I think you'd better make sure before they track you down, or Mother and Daddy arrive on Thursday. They're coming for the race on Saturday and staying for the wedding."

Richard hadn't seen his father in eight years. The thought of seeing him again made the balloon in his chest swell and his mouth water for the glass of wine he'd hardly touched at Thanksgiving dinner. The headache issued a few warning throbs. Richard took a swallow of his coffee, lit a cigarette and felt the pain ease.

Pickling his liver was obviously not acceptable, but it seemed to be perfectly okay to smoke himself into an emphysema ward. He'd have to report this to the surgeon general. If he didn't end up in a padded cell.

"Can I use your car this afternoon to pick up Devlin?"

"Sure. Look this over while I get the keys." She handed him the prospectus and left. Richard glanced through it, then puzzledly up at Meredith when she came back. "What I know about grain futures would fill the eye of a needle with room to spare," he told her. "Why did I read this?"

"So you'll know how I'm going to triple whatever money you have left in the next three months." She gave him the keys and sat in the desk chair. "Maybe quadruple."

"Why are you doing this, Meredith?"

"Because you need it and because I can." She smiled. "And because you're my brother, I'll waive my commission."

"I'm your stepbrother," he corrected her.

"You're my brother. *Period*," she said fiercely. "The only one I've got, which is a damn good thing, because I'm not sure I could survive another one."

When Susan smashed his nose all over his face, Meredith had been there to stop the bleeding and take him home. Now he was broke and here she was with grain futures. He wanted to tell her he loved her, but he couldn't, so he tipped up her chin and kissed her.

"Because I'm your brother," Richard told her, "I'll let you waive your commission."

"You're too kind," Meredith replied dryly.

"I know. Thanks for the car, step-brat. See you later."

One part of the dream still puzzled him—only half of him had gone after Susan. He couldn't figure out what had happened to the rest of him or what it meant, though he replayed the dream a dozen times as he drove into Santa Barbara. He looked under the pews in the church, in his grandmother's handbag, in the leaf-filled ditches edging the fields he raced across aboard High Brow in pursuit of Susan.

He didn't find himself—and he didn't catch Susan.

Richard tried not to let that trouble him, but it did, until Devlin got off the plane and he saw the black halo hovering above his snow-white head. Richard's blood turned to ice. He closed his eyes, opened them and looked again. The black cloud was gone. It was nothing, Richard told himself, just the reflection of Devlin's black overcoat. The book said that sometimes a person's aura would reflect colors.

Devlin saw him then, and put down the shopping bag and the battered pasteboard suitcase he carried. His cloudy blue eyes filled and his chin quavered as he held out his hand.

"Master Richard."

"Devlin." He checked the impulse to hug him and laid his hands on his shoulders instead. "I've known you all my life and I've never heard your first name."

"Devlin is my first name." He smiled, a murky twinkle in his eyes. "My surname is O'Roarke."

"Tough one to say when you're snockered," Richard replied with a grin.

"Precisely, sir."

"Well, listen up, Devlin O'Roarke. I'm going to take care of you from now on. I don't have a job yet or a hell of a lot of money, but we'll manage if you're game to try."

"But Master Richard." Devlin blinked at him. "I thought I'd come to take care of you."

"Not anymore." He picked up Devlin's suitcase and the shopping bag. "Is this all your luggage?"

"Yes, sir."

"Okay, then. Let's go home." It was a short walk to the Beemer, yet Devlin was puffing when they reached it. "You're overwarm. Let me take your coat."

"Thank you, sir, but I'm quite comfortable." Devlin closed one hand on the buttoned-up collar of his black coat. "I caught a bit of a chill on the plane."

Looking at the bright spots of color in Devlin's pale, almost chalky face, Richard also felt a chill. Foolishly he ignored it and helped him into the car.

On the drive to Cicada, he gave Devlin an encapsulated version of everything that had happened to him in the week since he'd left New York. Everything except the suspicion he was an empath or a lunatic, and that Susan knew and wouldn't help him. He didn't tell Devlin about the dream, either, or that he was pretty sure he'd fallen in love with Susan because she'd called him slugger. He figured that might tip the scales toward lunatic.

He knew it wasn't that simple. The moment she called him slugger was merely the moment of awakening, and he figured he had all the time in the world to explain to Devlin how he'd felt the first time he'd seen Susan in the foaling barn, why strong emotions scared the hell out of him and why he'd spent his life so far running away from them. Until now, until he'd found Susan and realized he'd never had the faintest damn idea what love was, that the little bit he knew about it he'd learned from him and Bea.

"Oh my," Devlin breathed, when Richard turned the Beemer through the Cicada Ranch gate, rounded the curve in the drive, and the house and the barns and the paddocks came into view.

"I know it's a far cry from Gramercy Park," Richard said, worried that Devlin would hate it here, "but the air's so clean you don't ever smell or see it. We don't have six locks on the door because we don't need them. You can see stars at night and you can drink the water that comes out of the tap and—"

"You don't need to sell me, sir. I'm already sold."

"But you haven't seen the house yet." Richard parked the BMW next to Loren Cade's old blue-and-rust Chevy pickup. "And the kitchen. Wait'll you see—"

"I don't need to see the kitchen." Devlin unfastened his seat belt and gave a tremulous smile. "Wherever you are, Master Richard, I shall be perfectly content."

Why hadn't Devlin told him this years ago, Richard wondered, and then realized that he had in a hundred different ways. When he'd taught him to tie his shoes, ride a bike and how to do long division.

"Me, too," Richard said, wishing he'd followed his impulse to hug Devlin at the airport.

He got out of the BMW and walked around it intending to do that very thing. He saw Meredith coming across the patio to meet them, opened the passenger door and held out his hand to help Devlin to his feet. Instead he caught him in his arms as Devlin tumbled, unconscious, out of the car.

20

"YOU CALL eleven thousand bucks an off day." Luke shook his head as Susan turned the Blazer off Highway 101 onto the two-lane blacktop leading toward home. "Amazing."

"I was distracted." Susan bent her elbow on the door and spread her fingers on her temple. She had been all day, but couldn't get a fix on why, other than it had something to do with Richard. "And tired because someone I know reneged on his offer to drive."

"Someone you know," he said, lifting his sunglasses to flash his two black eyes, "still thinks he has eight fingers on one hand."

"I can't wait to see how you explain those to Uncle Richard," Susan said, shooting him a quick grin.

"I'm gonna tell him the truth. His son the wuss dropped me with one punch. Let's see what he says about that."

"Don't expect miracles. Uncle Richard is an old dog and you know—" Susan clamped her left hand on the wheel and her right on her larynx to keep the scream that ripped suddenly through her head from tearing up her throat.

"All about old dogs and new—Jesus!" Luke clutched the armrest on the door to brace himself as the Blazer swerved hard toward the center line, then righted itself. "What's wrong, Suz?"

"I don't know." She gripped the wheel tightly in both hands, her throat throbbing. "Get Meredith on the mobile."

Luke did, fumbling the receiver of the phone tucked between the seats. Susan drew deep breaths to ease the tightness in her chest and the panic swirling through her—Richard's panic—and pushed the accelerator to the floor.

"Okay, cutie. Hang on." Luke pressed the phone to his chest. "I think she's hysterical. She said somebody named Devlin collapsed when he got out of the car."

"She's not hysterical." So that's what Richard's been up to all day, she thought. "Did she call 911?"

"Yes."

"Tell her we'll be there in ten minutes."

"Suz. Cicada is a good fifteen minutes from here."

"Tell her ten and hang on."

Susan made it in eight minutes flat, wheeling the Blazer into the far corner of the car park to give the ambulance and the paramedics plenty of room when they arrived. Someone had already moved Loren's truck and Meredith's BMW. Her father, most likely, her unflappable, practical old dad. Susan hit the ground running on rubbery legs with Luke half a stride behind her.

Her unflappable, practical and grim-faced dad met her at the back door. He closed a comforting hand on her arm, drew her quickly inside and across the mudroom.

"It don't look good, Susie. Heart attack, I'magine."

"What's the ETA on the ambulance?"

"Dispatch said fifteen minutes near twenty ago. Big crack-up on the interstate. Ever'body's tied up, 'cludin' the choppers."

"Where is he?"

"Guest room with Richard. He don't look good, neither. Won't let nobody near him. 'Cept you when you got here, he said. Richard ain't let go of his hand since he carried him in."

No wonder her chest hurt. Susan rubbed it, pushing ahead through the kitchen doorway. She paused long enough to catch her breath and saw Meredith, her face streaked with tears, throw herself at Luke. Then she raced down the hall toward the guest room with her father on her heels.

Outside the door she stopped, drew another deep breath and said calmly, as she stepped inside, "Don't let go of his hand, Richard. I'm here."

He knelt beside the bed holding Devlin's right hand in his left. He'd established that much of the link properly, receiving hand in sending hand. He'd done everything else right, too, to make it as easy as possible for Devlin's fluttering heart to pump—unbuttoned his overcoat, undone his collar and trousers and taken off his shoes, then covered his legs with a light blanket.

Richard lifted his head and looked at Susan. His face was chalky, his eyes almost black with agony.

"Help him," he said faintly. "He's in terrible pain."

So was Richard. It was etched in his voice.

"Holy Jesus," Loren breathed.

"Get my bag, Dad," Susan said, moving to the near side of the bed and dropping to her knees.

"Right here, Susie." He picked it up from the dresser and put it down on the floor beside her.

Susan's instruments were sized for horses, but worked the same as any doctor's. She listened to Devlin's heart with her stethoscope and took his erratic pulse. His pupils were dilated, his breath shallow and restricted.

Dropping the stethoscope around her neck, Susan looked at Richard over Devlin's laboring chest. He was breathing just as hard, his lips faintly blue. Asphyxia. God help her. She was a vet, not a cardiologist.

"He's fibrillating, which indicates an infarction, a blockage. I don't know how big or how bad."

"*Help him*," Richard ground at her between clenched teeth, anger flaring along with the agony in his eyes. "What you did for me, do for him."

"I'm going to, but first—"

"*Susie!*" Loren cried.

"Dad, I know what I'm doing." Susan silenced him with a sharp, warning look. "Call 911 and tell the dispatcher you want a chopper *now*. Clear a path for the stretcher and don't let anyone in here who isn't a paramedic."

Loren hesitated a minute, then squeezed her shoulder. "All right, Susie." He sighed, then left and shut the door.

But Susan didn't know what she was doing. Richard read it in her touch as she took Devlin's left hand in her right and his right in her left. What she'd done for him when he'd damn near knocked himself out with Luke was unique. She'd been able to help him because she'd known him so long and so well, but Devlin was different.

She didn't know him, not really, and she was a vet, not a doctor. Equine anatomy she knew like the back of her hand, but not human anatomy. And that was important. Maybe vital. He couldn't tell for sure because she was trying to block that from him.

"You've had the pain long enough, Richard." Susan squeezed his fingers, coaxing him to give it up. She felt her throat close, a vise clamp on her chest, but nothing else. "Give it to me now."

"No!" He gritted his teeth suddenly and threw back his head, the muscles and tendons in his neck clenching.

If Devlin were connected to an EKG the needle would be going crazy. Susan felt the old man's heart lurch, but just barely, for Richard abruptly yanked his hand out of hers, gave her a push to break her hold and gripped both Devlin's hands in his.

Ice-cold fear shot through Susan. He knew, dammit, he knew. She hadn't let her guard down, she knew she hadn't. He was simply that gifted; on a scale of one to ten about a thirteen. On her best day Susan ranked herself at seven, maybe eight.

"Let me help you." She tried, but couldn't break his grip on Devlin's hand.

"No." Richard closed his eyes tighter, let his head droop and panted for breath. Oh God, it hurt. Oh Christ! "Go away. I can do this."

"Not alone you can't. Let me in. Let me help."

"And risk killing you, too?" Richard flung his head up and looked at her. For just a second, fear and anger replaced the pain glassing his eyes. "Not a chance."

"You have to let me help you. You're taking the pain, but you aren't letting it go. You don't know how."

"Tell me."

"I can't. I have to show you."

"Forget it. I won't risk you, too."

"You're risking yourself."

"My choice."

"Listen to me, Richard." Susan wanted to scream at him, but kept her voice even. "It's not uncommon for a second attack to follow the first. If you don't let go of this pain and Devlin has another, you won't be able to save him. You'll be too weak. You could go with him."

"My risk." Richard blinked at her, sweat beaded on his deathly pale face. "My fight, Susan. Not yours."

"If you let me help I can release the pain and save you both. If you don't and it comes down to a choice, I can only save one." Susan held his gaze steadily. "And that will be *my* choice."

It was a brutal thing to say and Susan knew it. She didn't think it was possible, but Richard turned even paler. His eyes flicked from her face to Devlin's, then back again, brimming with tears.

"I can't!" The words tore out of him on a sob. He shut his eyes, but the tears fell anyway. They dripped off his chin and fell on Devlin's wrist. There was a tiny flinch of reaction, a good sign. "I can't let him die and I can't let you, either. Goddammit, Susan! *Goddammit!"*

He was shouting and sobbing—and at last letting go of the pain. Her nasty little trick had worked, Susan thought, with a sigh of relief. She closed her eyes, checked Devlin's pulse, felt it growing stronger and the pain shimmering off him in sick yellow waves. If the paramedics hurried....

A second before she heard the faint roar of the chopper she felt the hum of its vibration in the trembling window glass. She didn't think Richard heard it, but his head came up with a snap. His eyes were still swimming with tears, his lashes jeweled with them. He shot Susan a grin, a shaky, quavering grin that dissolved into fresh sobs when Devlin drew a breath, a deep, unlabored breath, and sighed.

Richard was still crying when the paramedics came shooting through the door with a stretcher and their equipment. He kept Devlin's hands for as long as he could, almost fell trying to get up out of their way, but managed to stay upright. Once Devlin was on oxygen and the medics had started an IV, Richard reclaimed the old man's right hand in his left and hurried along beside the chopper-bound stretcher.

Holding hands with her father, Susan ran along behind. Once they'd cleared the back door, the maelstrom stirred by the churning blades whipped her hair across her eyes. She hooked it behind one ear, saw Richard look back at her and lip-read his words: "I'm going with Devlin."

She knew better, but nodded. When Richard let go of Devlin's hand and stepped back so the medics could load the stretcher, he staggered, raised a hand to his forehead and took a drunken step toward the chopper. Susan and Loren rushed forward and caught him between them as he fainted.

21

WHEN RICHARD WOKE UP he was sprawled on his stomach in bed, Susan's bed. He knew it was hers because the eyelet trimmed pillow his face was buried in smelled like lavender.

For a god-awful five seconds, he thought he'd died and gone to heaven. Or slept through something he was going to kick himself for missing for the rest of his life.

In the next second he remembered Devlin, flipped over, shot up and looked Loren Cade in the eye across six feet of white down-filled silk comforter. He knew then that he hadn't missed a thing.

"How's Devlin?"

"Gonna be fine." Loren sat in a pink silk chair, one blue-jeaned knee crossed over the other. A crystal lamp on a brass-edged glass table illuminated the dog-eared copy of *Horse and Rider* he laid aside.

Stifling a yawn and shivering, Richard turned his head toward the west-facing window, a French door hung with white eyelet lace. Beyond its latticed panes the sky was nearly dark, just a few traces of deep mauve and purple were backlighting the hills ringing Cicada Ranch.

"Brave thing y'done this afternoon, Rich." Loren picked up his cigarettes from the table and lit one. "Mighty dumb, but brave."

"Story of my life, Loren." Richard raised his knees beneath the covers, bent his elbows against them and dragged his hands through his hair. "Toss me one, would you?"

"Don't know if I should." Loren snapped his lighter shut and blew smoke through his nose. "Seems t'me a fella recoverin' from a heart attack ain't got no business smokin'."

"Just gimme a cigarette."

"Glad t'see you ain't lost your sense of humor." Loren chuckled and tossed the pack and his lighter on the bed.

But he'd lost his shirt, Richard realized, as he stretched a bare arm to pick them up. His pants, too, he saw, when he peeked under the comforter. He lit a cigarette, closed his eyes and let the nicotine rush to his head.

Devlin would be all right. Thank God. But he'd be alone in a strange place. Richard took a second drag, tossed the covers aside and said, half expecting Loren to try to stop him, "I have to get to the hospital."

He saw why Loren didn't when he tried to stand and fell back on the bed. "Who took my knees? I want them back."

"'Magine you'll have 'em sometime tomorrow," Loren replied mildly, as he passed Richard an ashtray. "Don't fret about Devlin. Luke and Meredith went t'sit with 'im. He won't wake up alone not knowin' anybody."

Stuffing a pillow between his back and the brass headboard, Richard slid back under the comforter and eyed Loren Cade. He hadn't said a word about Devlin.

"Holy shit," he said slowly. "It runs in the family."

"Sure as hell don't grow on trees." Loren slouched in the chair and crossed his ankles. "I'm better at readin' thoughts. Susie's better at readin' feelin's."

"Holy shit," Richard repeated, wiping a hand down his face.

"Don't have a heart attack of yer own." Loren chuckled again and drew on his cigarette. "I don't make a habit outta tellin' folks I know what they're thinkin'. Ain't polite."

"But you know nonetheless." Richard dropped his hand and looked at Loren Cade. Really looked at him, for the first time seeing past his slow-talking, lopey-dopey cowboy facade.

"You ain't the first young fella been fooled by it." He laughed, then eyed Richard soberly. "Hope you plan on bein' the last, though, since you're in Susie's bed and I gotta feelin' she don't plan t'let you out of it any more'n you intend t'git out of it."

Richard barely managed to stifle the grin that wanted to jump all over his face. When Loren pointed his first and second fingers at him, his cigarette trailing blue smoke between them, he realized he might as well not have bothered.

"That's the problem with knowin' what's in folks' heads. Sometimes y'git confused and say somethin' y'shouldn't."

"Confused, my foot." Richard flicked the ash off his cigarette. "In answer to your question, cleverly disguised in cowpoke lingo, my thoughts are impure but my intentions are honorable. If Susan will have me."

"Good enough." Loren put out his cigarette and picked up Richard's robe from the padded brass stool at the foot of the bed. "I'm s'posed t'see you into the bathtub. No shower, Susie says, till you're steadier on your feet."

"Don't you want to know what changed my mind?"

"I already know you ain't got the foggiest damn idea. I'd try like hell t'come up with somethin' before Susie asks, though. Women set a lotta store by that kinda thing."

He'd tell Susan how he'd felt the first time he saw her in the foaling barn, Richard decided, as he soaked in her bathtub. Then he'd tell her about the dream. Then he'd tell her he loved her. He had no idea why or how, he just did. Then she'd break his nose. Then they'd kiss and make up. Then they'd—Richard jerked awake as his nose slid under water, shook his head and reached for a towel.

Maybe he'd just kiss her and take it from there.

He got out of the tub on his own, but Loren had to help him back to bed. Because he felt chilly he left his robe on, pulled the covers up to his chin and shivered as he watched Loren pour him a cup of cocoa out of a china pot that hadn't been on the table when he'd gone into the bathroom.

"Susie brung this," Loren said, handing him the cup. "Now she's fixin' dinner."

"W-why do I feel like this? D'you know?"

"Ran yourself dry, that's all. Drained your battery rechargin' Devlin."

Wishing it had marshmallows in it, Richard drank the cocoa and looked at Loren. "That sounds so simple."

"Ain't nothin' hard about it, Rich. Do b'lieve that's why most people don't git it and couldn't do it if they did."

"I don't remember much." Richard finished the cocoa and lit another cigarette. "I just—did—whatever I did."

His hand shook as he raised the cigarette to his mouth, but he wasn't cold anymore. Loren smiled and clapped a hand on his shoulder. A very gentle, fatherly hand.

"You ain't crazy, son. Just special." He gave him a wink and left the room.

In the nick of time, Richard thought, pressing his thumbs to his eyelids and the hot tears pricking behind them. He remembered crying, facedown on Devlin's chest, sobbing as if his heart would break. He'd wept in front of Susan, Meredith and Luke, Loren and the paramedics. And he couldn't care less.

It felt good. He remembered that, too. So damn good he was thinking about doing it again, until Susan kicked the door open.

"Hi, slugger." She wore a jungle-green silk dress and carried a washed oak lap tray. "Hungry?"

"I am now." Richard sat straight up, his mouth watering, not at the food but the dress. It wrapped around her like a second skin with only a skinny little belt tied in a bow at her left hip holding it together.

While he made short work of a thirty-two-ounce steak, salad, baked potato smothered in melted cheddar, green beans, gooseberry pie and a huge glass of milk, Susan sat watching him. When he finished, she took the tray to the kitchen, came back and sat facing him on the side of the bed.

"Devlin is in intensive care," she told him, "but it's precautionary. The doctor told Meredith it was a relatively mild attack. He can't rule out hypertension or disease until Devlin's well enough for tests, but at the moment he's inclined to think it was stress-induced."

"That's my fault." Richard looked guiltily away from Susan and picked up the cigarettes Loren had kindly left on the night table.

"Not entirely. He spoke to Meredith for a few minutes before they sedated him. Your grandmother fired him. He was supposed to be out tomorrow."

Watching Richard's eyes flare in the flame of her father's lighter made Susan's pulse leap. She strived to remain calm so he would, though she'd been seething since Meredith told her.

"That miserable old bitch," he said.

"She's your grandmother, Richard."

"So what?" He dragged on the cigarette and blew smoke through his nose, considered telling Susan she was in

Cancun with his mother and Alfreda, but didn't. He wasn't trying to withhold or evade anything, he just didn't want to think about the Weird Sisters. Let alone talk about them. "You said all I had to do was ask, Susan. Is that still true?"

"Yes." She ducked her chin and scratched at a cocoa splash on the white silk.

"Devlin's going to need a place to convalesce, and at the moment Cicada is the only one I have. I'll get a job and another place as soon as I can. Until then, can we stay here? I've got a few bucks to pay for our keep. 'Course, he'll have a hell of a hospital bill...."

Richard didn't expect an answer, he was just thinking out loud. His heart skipped as Susan lifted her eyes and looked at him, the lamplight giving her hair gleaming amethyst highlights.

"You have more than a few bucks," she said. "You have eleven thousand, three hundred and sixty-two dollars."

"I do?" Richard blinked at her. "Where'd I get it?"

"Luke and I went to Santa Anita today."

"Who staked me?"

"I did. The eleven, three sixty-two is yours clear."

"Why, Susan? I didn't ask you."

She looked down at the comforter again, the index finger of her left hand picking at something. Richard followed her gaze and saw the cocoa spot.

"You were right about the chip on my shoulder. I wanted to make that up to you, but mostly I wanted you to leave. You and Devlin are welcome to stay as long as you want, but you're free to go whenever you like."

Susan held her breath waiting for Richard to shout yippee, demand his money, jump out of bed, into his clothes and out of her house. Out of her life and out of her heart.

Richard's pulse was thudding in his throat, so loudly he was surprised Susan couldn't hear it. "Do you want me to leave?"

She raised her eyes to his face, amethyst glowing in her irises now. "No."

Lifting her hand from the comforter, Richard twined his fingers through hers. They were cold and trembling. He tipped up her chin with his right hand and felt his heart catch at the tears hanging like stars on her lashes.

"The first time I saw you I thought you were an angel. You had a halo."

"That was my aura." Susan sniffed. "I think you've always been able to see them if you'd let yourself, but—"

"It was a halo," Richard interrupted firmly. "A sunlight-and-straw-dust halo, and I thought you were the most beautiful thing I'd ever seen. I wanted you to touch me. I knew if you did I wouldn't feel empty and afraid anymore."

"Oh, Richard." Susan caught a shuddery breath. She lifted the back of her right hand to wipe her tears, but he beat her to it with his thumbs and gently cupped her face in his hands.

"That's when I fell in love with you. Right there, right then. I knew it, but I let my head talk me out of it, and it's been so messed up for so long that I—"

"You don't have to tell me. I know." Susan covered his hand with hers and touched her lips to his palm. The light, feathery kiss shot prickles of sensation across the nape of his neck.

"Probably better than I do, don't you?"

She smiled at him, her head turned slightly to one side, and said softly, "Probably."

"I do love you, Susan. I'm not doing a very good job of telling you, I know, but I'm trying. My head is still full of junk and I—"

"You don't have to tell me this, Richard." Susan put another kiss in his palm that almost melted his spine.

"I don't?" He blinked at her. "Loren said I did."

She laughed, so hard she rocked back on her tailbone.

"He said I better come up with a good one, 'cause women set a lotta store by this kinda thing."

Susan laughed harder, her eyes shining with fresh tears. "That's my dad," she sighed. "Crazy old Oakie."

"He's not crazy, Susan. Just special."

She blinked at him, wiping tears from her lashes with her curled index fingers. "He told you?"

"Now I understand why he slapped me around like a tennis ball every time he saw me. He was reading my filthy mind."

"It's the reason he drank."

"I figured that out when he told me. Maybe that's the reason I did." He stretched toward the nightstand and put out his cigarette.

Did, Susan repeated to herself, savoring the past tense.

Richard settled back on the pillows and looked at her. He didn't touch her, just caressed her with his eyes. They drifted past her face, lingered on her body, then lifted, reluctantly.

"So what am I? An empath or a lunatic?"

"Definitely an empath. Possibly a telepath. It's difficult to label you as one or the other because they bleed into each other, flow back and forth."

"Loren is a telepath, right? So what are you?"

"Both, like you. I'm very empathic, especially with horses. I always have been. Telepathic only sometimes and only with you. Usually I get feelings more than thoughts."

"How about now?" Richard asked with a devilish smile. "Can you tell what I'm feeling?"

"Yes." Susan took a breath to still her pulse, quickening in response to Richard's.

"Do you really think I've always been able to see auras?"

"Yes, but you didn't have anyone to tell you what they were. Perhaps you told someone who said you were silly, so you made yourself stop seeing them."

"I don't remember that," he said, thinking, trying to.

Susan remembered but didn't tell him, just eased up a wall in her head so he wouldn't see that she was seeing a very small Richard, chubby-kneed and towheaded, being jerked in the air by his grandmother swinging a belt and shouting at him it wasn't polite to point and how many times did she have to tell him. Susan had plucked the memory from his head at Foxglove a very long time ago. It still hurt her to remember it, and she was glad Richard couldn't.

"You had Loren to tell you you weren't crazy," he said.

"Yes."

Dear old Dad, always on hand to tell her things. It hadn't been fair of her to ask when he'd stopped in the kitchen on his way out, but she'd been so nervous. Was the dress too much? Too obvious?

"No flowers," he'd said, removing the bud vase with a single yellow rose in it from the tray. "Too sissy."

"It's symbolic," she'd said and flushed.

"You're sure this is what you want?" He'd lifted his hand and touched her chin then. "Not what Richard wants?"

"Yes, Dad," she'd told him firmly. "It's what I want."

"Okay." He'd picked up his Stetson and plunked it on his head. "You're a grown woman, so I'm gonna go home and watch TV. Mebbe play cards with Rufus, somethin' t'keep my mind off what's gonna be goin' on over here."

"I love you, Dad."

"Love you, too, Susie." He'd winked at her, turned to leave, then back again at her tremulous, "Dad? Did Richard say anything, or did you—"

"Susie." He'd tsked at her from the doorway, then smiled. "You should hear it from him, not me."

And she had, at long last. Even if he hadn't said he loved her, Susan would have known. Even without her gift. She saw it in his eyes, glowing in the lamplight, felt it in his touch when he lifted her hand and twined their fingers together.

"Why am I in your bed, Susan?"

"It's the biggest and the most comfortable and—"

"No, Susan," he interrupted her gently, "I mean why am I in it alone?"

22

"WELL, BECAUSE," Susan said, hoping her voice didn't sound as shaky to him as it did to her, "you haven't asked me to join you."

Richard caught the edge of the comforter and flipped it back. "I'm asking."

His black-and-gold silk robe gaped at the chest and was barely belted at the waist. It very plainly showed Susan where he was hard—and not so hard. His long legs were well-muscled and crossed at the ankle. The lamplight gleamed on his hair and made the gold stripes in his robe shimmer.

He was gorgeous, breathtaking, the happy ending to every dream she'd ever had, stretched out half-naked in her bed. It was too much. Susan didn't know where to look or what to do with her hands, so she clapped them over her eyes and said inside her head, *I'm-awake-I'm-awake-I'm-awake.*

Idiot, Richard cursed himself, springing up on his knees. You don't play flasher with a virgin.

"Susan, I'm sorry." He gently uncovered her eyes and held her hands. "I didn't mean to scare you."

"Oh, I'm not scared. I—" Susan's gaze strayed past his face. He had no hair on his chest at all, just flat bands of well-toned muscle. She wanted to touch him but forced herself to raise her head and look at him. "I feel like a princess in a fairy tale whose prince has just come."

He chuckled and leaned forward to nuzzle her ear. "Not yet, honey," he murmured, "he's waiting for you."

The laugh bubbling up in Susan's throat came out as a giddy moan as Richard traced his tongue around the shell of her ear. Shivers shot down her back and her arms as she lifted them to his shoulders and slipped them inside his robe. His skin felt warm and soft despite the hard muscle underneath.

"Candles," Richard whispered in her ear. "We gotta have lots of candles."

Susan pulled back and looked at him. "Why?"

"I've seen your hair and your eyes by candlelight," he said, cradling her face in both hands. "I want to see your body by candlelight while I make love to you."

Everything inside Susan fluttered. Richard closed his mouth over hers and kissed her, slowly and deeply. She had mush for bones when he lifted his head and smiled.

"How many?" she asked weakly.

"Dozen or so ought to do it."

"I'll get them."

"I will. Tell me where."

"The mantel, the dining room, my bathroom—"

"Don't move."

As if she could, Susan thought, sinking into a puddle on the bed. Candlelight. He wanted to see her by candlelight while he made love to her. Susan pinched herself. Yep. Still awake.

Richard came back with his arms full of candles, filled one nightstand with them, then the other. He lit them all, then turned off the lamp.

Susan pushed herself up and watched Richard strip off his robe. The candle flames filled the contours of his body with soft shadows and sharp angles as he tossed the robe on the bench and dropped to his knees in front of her. He slipped off her shoes and caressed her ankles, draped her legs over his shoulders, circled her waist with his arms and buried his face in her breasts.

Slipping her arms around his shoulders, Susan curled against him and laid her cheek on his hair. He smelled faintly of lavender sachet and soap. When he began to nuzzle her she caught her breath, at the scrape of his teeth across her nipples she whimpered.

Lifting his face, Richard looked into Susan's eyes. Flames flickered there, the ones he'd ignited with his touch, not Loren's lighter. Keeping his eyes on hers he softly cupped her breasts, saw her lashes flutter and her lips part. He nuzzled one, then the other, felt her heart pound beneath his ear, lifted his head and opened his mouth as she bent her head and kissed him.

She kissed him hungrily, thrusting her tongue past his teeth and raking her hands in his hair. He let her nip and suck at his mouth until he felt ready to explode. Then he opened the flap of her skirt and bared her legs to the cooler air. She shivered and broke the kiss, threw back her head, sighed and spread her legs when he ran his hands up her thighs.

"Susan." He kissed the inside of her knee, nuzzled with his nose and heard her moan. "We have to slow down." He nuzzled her other knee, tracked a long, wet kiss up her thigh and felt her melt into the bed on her back. "Hear me, Susan? I said we have to slow down."

Then he reached for the skinny little bow belt and found it already undone. He glanced up at Susan who was watching him with a dewy-eyed smile.

"I thought I'd untie it," she said dreamily, "before I lost complete control of my motor functions."

Laughing softly in his throat, Richard sat up on the bed beside her. She stretched her arms over her head, so that when he laid the halves of her dress open her breasts swelled above the cups of the flimsiest excuse for a brassiere he'd ever seen.

"Dr. Cade." He made a playful shocked gasp. "Do your patients know you own underwear like this?"

"Since my patients don't," she said, with a laugh that rippled her soft curves and made Richard groan. "I assume they couldn't care less."

Bending over her on one elbow, he kissed her, then murmured against her mouth, "I want to see all of you, Susan." He kissed her again while he slid the dress off her arms and her panties down her legs, and opened the front snap of her bra with one deft flick of his fingers. He didn't look until he'd freed her arms of the straps, and when he did—

"Oh God, Susan." Richard closed his eyes, rested his forehead against hers and swallowed hard. "You're even more beautiful than I thought you would be."

"Look who's talking," she murmured, running the tip of one finger along his jaw.

He caught her hand and kissed it, pressing everything he felt into her palm. How beautiful she was, how funny she could be, how giving and generous.... He lifted his head to look at her when he felt an answering tingle in his own palm and knew that to Susan he was the handsomest man she'd ever laid eyes on, that she'd loved him from the moment she'd seen him—when he wasn't so handsome, how intelligent she thought he was, how debonair he looked in tweed, how she wanted him to—

"Susan!" The shock he felt was genuine. Not at her luscious suggestion, but that she'd put it in his mind somehow.

Stunned as he was, he did what she wanted, bent his head to her lush left breast and swirled his tongue around her nipple. She moaned and arched, thrusting more of her into his mouth. He took her and sucked, cupped and kneaded her and almost lost his mind and his control when he knew how it felt to Susan.

"Oh Jesus, Susan." Richard pressed his forehead to hers again. "How do I know how that feels to you?"

"I wanted you to."

He lifted his head and looked at her. "That's it? That how?"

"Mmm-hmm."

Richard's heart started to pound. "Can I make you feel what I feel?"

"You've always been able to."

He grinned wickedly. Susan's eyes widened. It was tempting, but . . .

"On second thought, maybe tomorrow," he decided, sliding down beside her. "Tonight's just for you."

"Why can't it be for us?"

"Because this is your first time and I want it to be special."

"It is special. I'm with you."

"Don't tell me you saved yourself for me."

Susan smiled. "What d'you think?"

"I think I'm one lucky son of a bitch." He grinned while she laughed, then he kissed her nose. "I've never been with a virgin."

"What a coincidence. Neither have I."

"I don't have to explain the technicalities, do I?"

"No." Susan's eyes gleamed with candle glow and the corners of her mouth twitched. "I've been to vet school."

Then she laughed, and in spite of himself, Richard grinned. "I'm trying to be serious. I don't want to hurt you."

"Listen to me, Richard." Susan closed his chin in her hand. "You never meant to, I know, but you've spent the past fifteen years hurting me. You can erase it all, forever, by shutting your mouth, taking what I saved for you and making all my dreams come true."

"I've never been anybody's dream," Richard told her, his voice thick in his suddenly tight and aching throat.

"Yes, you have. You just didn't know it." Susan gave him a soft, openmouthed kiss, then a narrow, warning look. "But you're rapidly turning into a nightmare, slugger."

"Well, in that case," Richard chuckled, lacing his fingers through hers and stretching her arms over her head. "Batter up."

23

"RICHARD, WAKE UP. I need you. *Hurry*."

"Again?" he muttered groggily, rocking back and forth with the mattress as Susan shook him. "So soon?"

Talk about a dream come true.

"Not *that*." Richard felt the bed lurch as Susan sprang off it. "Peggity's foal is coming. I may need your help."

"What?" He shot up on his hands, bleary-eyed but awake. "Miss Scarlett, I don't know nothin' 'bout birthin' no babies."

"You'll learn." She was already into her underwear and was yanking a pair of jeans out of a dresser drawer as she flung a frantic look at him. "Please, Richard. If that inflamed fetlock gives her trouble I'll need all the help I can get."

His special kind of help. Susan didn't say it, but she didn't have to.

"I'm your man," he said, shooting to his feet.

"I know," she said with a smile.

Richard couldn't find his glasses, forgot them, threw on jeans and a sweatshirt in the guest room, grabbed Susan's bag and met her in the hall. They locked hands and raced through the dark toward the foaling barn. Halfway there, they heard the other mares whickering nervously.

In a flash, Susan had the lights on. The bay mare and the two chestnuts stood alert, their ears up and their heads angled toward the back of the barn. A step behind Susan, Richard rounded the turn and looked into Peggity's stall.

The mare was down, not rolling, which was common enough in labor, but flailing to get up.

"Oh, *Peggity*." Susan bolted to her side, fell to her knees and laid a hand on her neck. The mare quieted almost instantly. Susan glanced up and nodded for Richard to come into the stall. "Come up here and talk to her while I look her over."

Richard did what he was told, replacing Susan's hand on the mare's neck with his own. Peggity rolled an eye at him and flared her nostrils. The first touch gave him a jolt, as it had when he touched High Brow. He stroked her neck and crooned while Susan snapped on a glove and did an internal exam.

"Dammit," she said, "one leg is bent and stuck on the pelvis. We've got to get her up so I can turn the foal."

Peggity tried gamely to stand at least half a dozen times, but gave it up as soon as she put any weight on to the badly inflamed fetlock. Richard and Susan did what they could to help her, but it was futile.

"Can't you straighten the foal with her down?"

"No. There's too much pressure and not enough room." Susan shook her head and chewed her lip. "We'll have to think her on her feet. Convince her there's nothing wrong with that fetlock, that it doesn't hurt and she can stand."

Ought to be a snap after a heart attack, Richard thought. "What do you want me to do?"

"Change places." He moved to the mare's rear quarters and Susan to her head. "Now put your hands on her ankle. Right above the fetlock. Picture in your mind no swelling, no pain. Think a sound leg. Can you do that?"

"I can try." Richard dropped to his knees and put his hands where Susan told him, felt the heat in the leg and the pain. "Then what?"

"When she shifts to get up, don't let go. Keep your hands on her leg. She won't think to kick you, she'll be too busy birthing the foal."

Susan hoped she wouldn't kick. Richard heard the afterthought, but pretended he didn't.

"You might see some really weird stuff. Horses have very different minds. Don't get distracted. Keep thinking a sound leg. And don't pay any attention to me. I'll be moving around a lot."

Sound leg, sound leg. Richard thought it, closed his eyes and made a picture of one, bay like the mare, in his mind. No swelling, no pain. He felt another jolt, saw blindingly brilliant three-dimensional colors and shapes inside them, pushed them away and focused on a sound leg with no pain and no swelling. The colors spun behind the image, focused and shifted into sky, rolling clouds and wind.

He felt it, tasted it, concentrated on no swelling, no pain. The wind tore through his hair, lifted and streamed over his withers. *Oh Lord.* Panic flared, but Richard clamped down on it and thought sound leg, no pain, no swelling.

He felt lather—*no, sweat, dammit*—on his forehead, on his flanks. *Oh God.* Sound leg, no pain. His legs moved like pistons, driving him faster, faster. He ran with the wind. No pain, no swelling, sound leg. *God please, no pain, no*— He was the wind. He was born to race with it, outrun it if he could, be part of it for as long as his legs could drive him, until his heart burst with the sheer joy of running....

"*Richard!*" Susan's voice snapped like a whip. "Sound leg. No pain. No swelling. Sound leg. No pain—"

No swelling. He had it back and clung to it, focused on it with every ounce of strength he had, afraid that if he lost it he'd lose himself in those glorious colors, the smell and the feel of the wind. He felt the mare shift and rolled on his side to keep his hands in place. No pain, sound leg, no swelling. He heard her snort, felt the tendons in her leg tense to step and held on for dear life. No swelling, no pain, no swelling. *Please God, don't let her kick me.* Sound leg, no pain.

Peggity's tail lashed the side of his face. Richard opened one eye and saw Susan slide her arm inside the mare to straighten the foal. He closed his eyes again and concentrated when Peggity's leg tensed again. He tried to hold her, but couldn't. She took a dragging step with his fingers clamped on her ankle. Sound leg, no—

"Richard! Let go and open your eyes. Now!"

He did, managing to swing himself out from under the mare's belly a half second before her foal plopped into his lap. Her very heavy foal. The breath went out of him, but he sucked it back and gaped at the foal, alive and moving, thrusting its head through its sac to breathe.

"Sit still," Susan said, needlessly, as Peggity turned her head, swung her quarters around and began to nose and lick the foal.

Its little hooves dug into him as it flailed to stand. Richard leaned back out of the way, until Peggity lifted her head, fixed an eye on him and snorted.

You could help, you know.

Richard shot an amazed look at Susan. "Did she—"

She shrugged, smiled and tossed him a soft piece of chamois cloth. Gingerly, until he was sure Peggity would allow it, he rubbed the foal. Then more energetically, giving gently encouraging boosts.

At last, when Richard thought his legs would break, the foal clambered off him onto its feet, switched its tiny tail and smacked him in the face. Clapping a hand over his stinging right eye, he watched the foal wobble to Peggity's teat and start to nurse. The mare turned to watch with a satisfied whicker, then swung her head toward Richard, nuzzled his hair and snorted.

Thanks, slugger.

Overcome with exhaustion and wonder at what he'd seen and felt, Richard collapsed on his back, arms outflung in the straw. What a day. What an incredible day.

"Nice lookin' filly y'got there, Rich."

Tilting his head back, he saw Loren leaning on his elbows on the stall door. "Yeah, I know," he said, shifting his gaze to smile at Susan.

"I meant the foal, son."

"It's a girl?" Richard watched the baby nurse, then shot a triumphant look at Susan. "It's a girl! Our first!"

"Flagmaster's, too," she said with an indulgent smile.

"No kidding." Grinning like a goof, Richard sprang up on one hand. "Why, that old devil."

"Seems t'me," Loren said, "such a special little filly deserves a special name. Since Rich brung her into the world, I think he deserves the honor. You, Susie?"

"Absolutely."

"Anything I want?" Richard asked Loren over his shoulder. "I don't have to come up with one of those dopey eighteen character combinations of the name of the sire and dam?"

"Nope. Anything you want."

Richard looked at Peggity and the foal and pronounced her, "Sirocco."

"Desert wind," Susan murmured. "I like it."

"Me, too," Loren agreed.

Father and daughter exchanged a secret smile that told Richard they'd been where he'd been, seen and felt what he'd seen and felt. Loren had tried to tell him. He remembered that now, remembered what he'd said as they'd sat by the fire after supper his first night at Cicada, "If a hoss runs for the sheer joy of runnin', he'll run 'til his heart bursts. Same with a woman, son. Same with a woman."

He looked up at Susan again, her glorious hair shimmering in the bright overhead lights, caught her eye and felt a warm glow of joy and contentment spread from his solar plexus. Richard's throat swelled and tears welled in his eyes. He belonged. At long, blessed last he belonged.

What a day. What an incredible day.

"I'm not finished yet," Susan said. "You fellas might as well go on to bed."

"Not without you." Richard pushed to his feet, saw the flush on Susan's face and turned toward Loren.

His face was as red as his daughter's hair, but he was grinning, too.

While Susan monitored the delivery of the afterbirth and gently examined Sirocco, Richard and Loren cleaned the soiled straw out of the stall and spread fresh. Once dam and foal were cleaned up and content, they left the barn, shutting the lights out as they went.

The first traces of dawn were streaking the sky above the eastern hills. Loren was yawning, Susan rubbing the back of her neck tiredly, but Richard was wired, flying so high he thought he'd never come down.

At the bungalow, Loren left them. Richard put his arm around Susan, felt hers slip around his waist and her head settle against his shoulder. She smelled like lavender and horse, blood and sweat. He felt his throat swell again and kissed the top of her head.

When they reached her bedroom, she fell, spread-eagled, already asleep on the bed. Richard tugged off her boots, his Nikes, crawled in beside her, rolled her into his arms with her head on his chest and pulled the comforter over them.

Susan stirred, but only slightly, just enough to hear the thrum of Richard's heart beneath her ear, then she snuggled against him and slept. A deep, and for the first time that she could remember, dreamless sleep. She woke up to sunlight pouring across the room and the digital clock staring her in the face. Nine-twenty.

"You're not late," Richard said. "I called Luke and told him you and I were up half the night—"

"You didn't!" Susan cried, flipping over to look at him, leaning on one shoulder in the bathroom doorway, his robe knotted loosely at his waist.

"—delivering Peggity's foal," he finished with a grin.

Susan grabbed a pillow and threw it at him. He ducked. When she threw the second one, he caught it, and told her over the eyelet-trimmed hem, "Keep this up and I won't make love to you in your bubble bath."

"You can't do *that* in a bubble bath."

"My darling Susan. I can do *that* anywhere. On a Fifth Avenue bus if the mood strikes." Richard pushed himself off the door frame with one hand. "As a matter of fact, I think I did once."

Susan laughed. Richard held out a hand to her. Throwing back the comforter, she got out of bed and went to him.

"Take a few minutes." He put a kiss on her nose, pushed her into the bathroom, pulled the door half shut and raised his eyebrows suggestively. "Then I'll show you what I can do in a bubble bath."

Dreamily Susan drifted to the sink to brush her teeth, got a good look at herself in the mirror and froze with her hand on her toothbrush. Good lord. He'd kissed that face with the ruined mascara and the hair sticking up around it like straw. He must love her.

Once she was brushed, washed and wrapped in a towel, Susan opened the bathroom door and crooked a finger at

Richard lounging on the bed. He got up, shrugged off his robe and walked toward her. She felt her face flame with a rush of embarrassment and desire. In the doorway, Richard cupped her face and kissed her.

"Don't be shy," he murmured, his voice husky. "I love you and you love me. It's okay to look at my body. Even better if you enjoy it."

"Oh I do," Susan sighed.

While he filled the bath, dumping oils and crystals willy-nilly, Susan sat on the lid of the toilet and watched him. When he slid into the tub and held out a hand to her, she rose and dropped her towel. She wasn't sure she could ever be as easily naked around Richard as he was with her, but the expression on his face made her consider giving it a try.

The water like silk on her skin, Susan settled herself between Richard's legs, sighed, and leaned her back against his chest. He drew a deep breath in her ear, cupped her breasts in handfuls of suds and nibbled her earlobe. Ecstatic shivers shot everywhere.

The bubbles lasted all of two minutes.

By the time the last one popped on her left shoulder, Susan was facing Richard, her legs spread over his, his mouth on her breasts. The flick of his tongue shot slivers of sensation through her. She cupped his head to her, arched her throat, lost her grip on the bottom with her slippery knees and felt him slide deep inside her.

"Ohhh," she gasped, amazed that you *could* do this in a bubble bath.

"I'm all yours." Richard leaned back against her terry bath pillow and cupped her hips in his hands. "Take what you want."

Susan did, lost in the silken slide of the water around her and Richard inside her. When he began to move with her, the water lapped around them, sloshing over the side, but neither of them noticed. Neither of them cared.

They belonged to each other in the best way, and in a very special way few other people could ever understand.

24

AFTER THEY GOT OUT of the bubble bath and Susan left for Roundhouse, Richard paid a visit to Flagmaster. Complete with a carrot he kiped from Consuella and a cigar he mooched off Rufus.

Bravely he climbed the fence and sat on the top rail. It took the old devil a couple minutes to realize Richard was there, but when he did he came on the charge with his ears flat against his head.

"Before you tear my leg off," Richard called calmly, though his heart was remembering in vivid detail what he'd gone through with Devlin, "I think you should know I helped deliver your daughter last night."

The stallion skidded to a halt. One ear flicked forward. He turned his head warily to the side and rumbled.

"Yeah, a girl." Richard stuck the cigar in his mouth, lit it, puffed and blew smoke at Flagmaster. The stallion snorted and shook his head. "Stinks, I know, but it's tradition."

Flagmaster turned his head the other way and flicked his ears again.

"None for you, eh? Okay. How's this?" He pulled the carrot out of his back pocket, broke it in two and held out a half on his flattened palm. "Cigar for me. Carrot for you."

The stallion began to drool. Susan had told him he loved carrots. It took him a good five minutes to take the first hesitant step, another three to take four or five more, but finally he came close enough to snuffle Richard's hand, drool all over his fingers, snatch the carrot, wheel away and pulverize it in his teeth. It only took him half as long to take the rest.

"Well, that's it. Congratulations, old man." Richard swung his legs over the fence to climb down, then paused. "Oh, by the way. Should I ever happen to stumble into your space again—and believe me, I'll try like hell not to— you'll remember the carrot and the happy tidings I brought and not kill me, won't you?"

Flagmaster gave him a don't-press-your-luck snort.

"Nice talking to you." Richard jumped down from the fence with the cigar in his teeth, turned around and found himself nose to nose with a very pale-faced Loren Cade.

"Son, lemme explain a couple things to you." He laid a heavy hand on Richard's shoulder. "Number one, you're mortal. Number two, that stallion is one mean son of a buck. There ain't no playin' nice horsey with Flagmaster. He just loves fools like you to bring him carrots and git close enough he can stomp you into the ground. Number three, Susie loves you. Truth be told, I'm developin' a soft spot for you m'self. Don't wanna see her a widow 'fore she's a bride."

"He just seems so lonely." Richard looked back at Flagmaster, rubbing his jaw on the top rail of the fence. "I kind of got the feeling he's been mistreated."

"You're right there. Just like people, hosses ain't born mean, they're made mean." Loren looped an arm around Richard and drew him away from the paddock. "Now, about Susie bein' a bride. When you s'pose that might be gonna happen?"

He told Loren, and he told Susan that night—sort of— once he'd made love to her and they were sitting up in bed on pillows. Her eyes shone when he put a blue velvet ring box in her hand.

"I bought this today after I visited Devlin, while I waited for my new contacts. It's not a diamond." He stayed her hand as she started to open it. "Not until all the hoopla with Meredith's wedding is over and done with. I don't want you to eclipse her."

Susan opened the box and caught her breath. A pear-shaped amethyst dotted with diamond chips winked at her.

"Oh Richard. It's beautiful," she said, giving him an openmouthed kiss as he slipped the ring on her finger. "The same color as my aura."

"That's why I bought it," he said, letting his gaze drift from her face to the top of her head. "Which by the way, is almost purple at the moment. Normally it's only purple when I'm in—"

"C'mere, you," she laughed, hooking her arm around his neck and dragging him under the covers.

Susan spent the next three days looking at her left hand every ten seconds, shopping with Meredith to buy something stunning to wear in the winner's circle on Saturday and generally floating ten feet off the ground. Even when Satan, crankier than usual about his diet, tried to bite her again, she merely kissed him on his gray-speckled nose.

Every day, to fill the hours Susan spent at Roundhouse, Richard visited Devlin and Sirocco. She fascinated him, her dark little eyes bright as buttons as she gamboled around Peggity in their stall. Falling and getting up, looking startled when she fell again, swinging her head around as if to say, "Who tripped me?" There were secrets in her eyes, secrets about the wind Richard ached to know.

On Tuesday he helped Susan load Banner into the P. H. Cade Racing Stable horse van and drive him to Roundhouse, where he'd be stabled and worked to get used to the track before Saturday's race. For the very first time, he and Luke had an honest-to-God conversation.

After dinner on Wednesday night, he went with Susan to the foaling barn to check on Sirocco. She came to the stall door, little bottle-brush tail switching, cocked her head at them and whinnied in her tiny, tinny little voice.

Richard adored her and the woman beside him. "I want you," he murmured to Susan. "Right here, right now." Then he took her into the next stall, shut the top door, spread a horse blanket and ravished her at length.

The next day, Thursday, Richard Senior arrived with Bea.

Unlike Devlin, he hadn't changed much in eight years. A bit more gray at his blond temples that turned silver in the glorious sunshine as he helped Bea out of the BMW. Standing in the patio holding Susan's hand, Richard watched them walk toward the house and realized, for the very first time, that physically he was the image of his father.

Susan had always seen it, but felt the jolt of surprise in his fingers. She gave them a reassuring squeeze, and Richard an extra shot of courage. Not that he needed it. Like the little soldier his father had raised him to be, he stepped forward and gripped his hand. Perhaps a bit too firmly, Susan thought, noticing her uncle flinch slightly.

"Well, Susan," he said expansively, as usual dismissing Richard as soon as he could, "let's have a tour of the stables, shall we?"

"Sure, Uncle Richard." She slid Richard a "wanna come?" look, but he shook his head.

Then he gave her a wink and mouthed a kiss he thought no one else saw, until he and Bea, still petite and blond as ever, were alone in the kitchen after lunch. She took his face in her hands, pulled him down and gave him a teary-eyed smack on his mouth.

"I saw you blow that little smooch at Susan, you big, handsome lug. You deserve her."

"I think we deserve each other," Richard told her with a smile.

Luke came to supper, which Richard Senior completely monopolized. It infuriated Richard, but no one else seemed to mind. Not even Loren, who usually presided at the table. He merely slouched in his chair wearing his lopey-dopey cowboy grin.

Watching him, Richard felt his fury drain away. At least two of them knew his father for what he was. Still, he couldn't resist getting even, and dragged Bea to her mother's cherry spinet during coffee and drinks after dinner.

They played and sang the way they used to on those bleak winter afternoons at Foxglove, chasing each other's fingers over the keyboard trying to outdo each other. When Susan came with the carafe to freshen Bea's cup, he played the first four bars of "Someday My Prince Will Come."

Susan's cheeks flamed but her heart swelled. He was having a wonderful time playing one-up on his father—and winning, though he hadn't a clue. Absorbed in the music and Bea's radiant company, he was completely unaware that his fingers hadn't stumbled once on the keys, that Richard Senior was listening, really listening, that his eyes were actually glistening.

Carrying the server back to the dining room, Susan put it down on the sideboard and smiled. Life, she thought, was sweet. When she turned around, Meredith was there. They grinned and gave each other a high five.

She gave Richard one later, after he'd outdone himself, then wheedled him out of bed with lewd promises she swore to keep if *only* he'd bring her a bologna sandwich and a glass of chocolate milk. For the things Susan said she'd do, Richard would have walked through fire.

He was on his way back to her, whistling under his breath, happily sloshing milk down the front of his robe, when his father stepped out of the second guest room in his pajamas. In the hallway, lit only by the wedge of light behind Richard Senior, they froze and stared at each other. His father recovered first, shot a look at Susan's bedroom door, then at Richard, and squared his shoulders.

"Is this what I think it is?" he demanded.

"I don't know, Dad," Richard challenged. "What do you think it is?"

His father opened his mouth, shut it, then said, "None of my damn business," stepped back in the guest room and shut the door.

Life was sweet, Richard thought, and grinned.

He continued to think so until Saturday, right up to race time. He hadn't had any dreams, no more visits from the Ghost of Christmas That Never Was, not so much as the teeniest inkling that anything was amiss, no hint whatsoever that apocalypse awaited him at Roundhouse.

Even on an off day, the place looked magnificent. Today it shone with fresh paint, tubs of potted flowers everywhere, red-and-white-striped pavilions dotting the grounds around the mile dirt track. Richard had been to Ascot, but had never seen anything like this.

The grounds were mobbed with the cream of Santa Barbara society. There were diamonds and furs and money everywhere, even in Richard's pocket, which he touched as he squired Meredith, dressed in a tea-length sky blue suit with matching wide-brimmed hat, into one of the tents and procured two glasses of champagne from a bubbling fountain.

"To you, step-brat," he said, toasting her. "A lot of little kids are going to be very happy because of you."

"It's great, isn't it?" Meredith clinked her glass against his and sipped. "I'd hoped for a good turnout, but I never dreamed anything like this."

"Dreams don't do you much good," he reminded her, "if they don't come true now and then."

"Tripped by my own foot." Meredith laughed, sipped some more, then gave Richard a slow once-over.

"What's wrong? Is my fly open?"

"No." Meredith made a face at him. "I've been taking notes and comparing, that's all, and I've decided that of all the men here in morning coats, you look the best."

"Don't let Dad hear you say that."

Meredith laughed again as he took her elbow and steered her outside, into the glorious California sunshine, the high rolling, immaculately dressed crowd—and straight into the face of doom. Meredith saw them first, stumbled to a halt on Richard's arm and blanched.

"Run," she said, pushing him and splashing champagne on his arm. "Hide. Levitate. Disappear."

"Hey, step-brat. Hold it." Brushing wine off his sleeve, Richard looked up and saw his mother through the crowd about twenty yards away.

25

SHE DIDN'T SEE HIM, thank God. Neither did his grandmother, stalking boldly behind her with her cane in one hand and—what else?—a highball in a clear plastic cup in the other.

Every purple hair on Mrs. Barton-Forbes's head, and there weren't that many, was combed to perfection. The sapphires and diamonds his grandfather had given her on their fortieth wedding anniversary glittered in her droopy ears and circled her sagging throat. She was sixty-eight and looked eighty.

Alfreda slunk along beside her, looking down her patrician nose at the bourgeois Americans. Her blond hair was swept beneath a big-brimmed hat that matched her miniskirted royal-purple suit and the dyed-to-match fur piece sloping off one shoulder. She was a stunner, maybe a nymphomaniac and every inch a bitch.

So was his mother. A spoiled, petulant, haughty bitch. Yet he loved her, despite all her tricks and deceits and indifference. So much he ached watching her sweep ahead of his grandmother and Alfreda in a dramatic black coatdress trimmed in ermine that must've cost Sir Freddie a good chunk of his quarterly allowance.

At her throat and wrists diamonds flashed among pearls. The pin in the boat-size hat slanting over one side of her face sported a rock the size of his thumbnail. He had her nose, Richard realized, studying her face through the dotted net veil covering her eyes, but nothing else of hers, thank God.

Her full mouth was drawn in a thin, impatient line. Her green eyes darted ceaselessly back and forth. When they moved toward him, Richard felt his heart freeze in his chest.

This was his dream. Not a nightmare at all, but another scrambled premonition. A warning he hadn't paid any attention to. He realized it, then did what any sensible man would do—he grabbed Meredith's arm and ran like hell in the opposite direction.

"Where's Susan?"

"In the paddock with Uncle Loren, saddling Banner."

"I've got to warn her."

"Richard." Meredith stopped and jerked him around to face her. "You didn't *tell her* they were on the hunt for you?"

"No, I didn't. And don't give me that look. Something else kept coming up."

"Let me guess what."

"Find Bea." Richard gripped her shoulders. "She's a better-than-even match for my mother. Then find Dad. Make sure you pour at least a magnum of champagne down him *before* you tell him my mother's here. I'll handle Susan."

"Good luck." Meredith slapped a hand on her hat and shot off into the crowd.

Son of a bitch, Richard swore, ducking and sidling around knots of people, running when he could down the slope toward the track. The rails were already lined with spectators, in some places three or four deep. He should've told Susan when he had the chance.

He wished he had and wished the crowd would disappear, almost as much as he wished he could wish the Weird

Sisters back to Cancun. When people weren't laughing and talking and drifting across his path, they were stopping or swinging around abruptly in front him. Their faces were a blur of teeth and eyes, flashy jewels and outlandish hats.

The call to the post sounded, shooting chills up Richard's back. He lurched out of the crowd at the paddock rail, nearly went over it headfirst, pulled himself back and saw Banner's black-and-white tail switching as he walked sedately through the gate and down a makeshift ramp toward the track behind dancing, prancing High Brow.

He saw grooms and dignitaries, photographers and socialites, but no Susan. Where in hell was she? He wanted to scream her name but didn't, just pushed back into the crowd, frantic for a glimpse of her amethyst silk suit he'd wanted to peel her out of when he'd seen her in it that morning. He shoved his way toward the track, certain she'd be there.

She wasn't.

Susan! He shouted her name in his head, raked his fingers through his hair. *Darling Susan, where are you?* He caught a vague snatch of her, a whisper of amethyst in his head, but couldn't pinpoint it. Dammit, where was she?

Cursing, he struck off again into the crowd. He didn't see Susan anywhere, but he saw Bea in the distance at the entrance to one of the pavilions. For all of three seconds she blocked his mother's path, until Lady Simpson gave her an out-of-my-way-peon shove, into a table and a tray full of champagne-topped glasses. They fell like ninepins, soaking her pink Dior suit, but she waved Richard away as he caught her eye, set her jaw, tugged her blush-dyed mink around her shoulders and struck off in hot pursuit of Lady Simpson and her entourage.

Richard heard the gun and the starter's "They're off!" through the public address system set up for the occasion. The crowd roared and he ran—ran to find Susan, to shield her and love her for the rest of her life. And his, if she didn't kill him.

The black colt and the chestnut filly flew neck and neck into the first turn, legs and hearts pumping, the wind—*oh the wind*—streaming past them. Richard caught in the link sensed it in his head—the straining, driving to outrace the wind.

The winner's circle. Fool! He smacked a hand against his forehead. She'd know and she'd be there.

Whirling in the opposite direction, Richard ran, but not as fast as Banner and High Brow, running as one down the backstretch into the far turn, stride for stride challenging each other and challenging the wind.

Oh the wind. If only he could run like the wind.

On the rail High Brow came thundering first into the home stretch, a spray of loam flying in her wake. On the outside came Banner, a whole length lost in the turn.

The crowd roared again and Richard whirled toward the track. Over the bobbing heads in front of him, he caught a glimpse of High Brow shooting past, her red mane whipping. On her flank raced Banner, nostrils flared, straining to outrace her and catch the wind.

On his back a green-and-blue arm raised a whip that never fell, for the wind and his sire's fiery love of the chase caught the black colt. Richard felt the jolt in a blinding flash of color in his head and saw Flagmaster—just for an instant, only for a heartbeat—racing the fence in his paddock at Cicada. He felt more than saw the essence of the flying black stallion meld with that of his son. Red superimposed on blue swirled together in Richard's head as Banner's neck stretched, his stride lengthened and he flew, one with the wind at last, in a lathered black blur past the streaming red filly.

In the winner's circle, Susan jumped into her father's arms. She and Loren clung together laughing and crying until Susan's ribs hurt from the strength of his embrace. When she turned, Banner was prancing toward her, silver bolts of lightning shooting through his electric-blue aura.

At his head, holding his bridle and leading him, Rufus grinned ear to ear. On his back, his chin strap loose and his face streaked with sweat and dirt, Paulie O'Gilbert shook his whip in the air. His face glowed with triumph, then crumpled into tears as he threw himself forward and hugged Banner's wet black neck.

"Ain't that nice," her father said, his voice choked.

"It would be a lot nicer if Richard—" In mid-sentence, Susan turned her head to look for him and saw Lady Simpson.

Then Richard's grandmother behind her with Lady Alfreda.

Their presence cut like a knife through Susan's euphoria. She felt the way she had in London, at Epsom, when she'd raised the binoculars and looked at Lady Alfreda. Ugly and gauche. There was no chain around Lady Alfreda's neck, and no ring but the one on Susan's finger. She looked down at her hand, at the amethyst winking in the sunlight.

"Steady, Susie," her father said behind her, his hands closing on her shoulders. "Don't jump the gun here."

"I won't," she said, but she wanted to.

Just as she had in London, she wanted to run off the racecourse, but didn't. Richard had stopped running and so had she. Whatever happened she'd stand here and take it. For courage, she turned the ring on her hand and closed her fist around the amethyst.

"Dammit to hell," Richard Senior said, bumping into Susan as he lurched out of the crowd beside her with Meredith tugging on his right arm and Bea on his left. "She *is* here."

Lady Simpson saw him then and raised her chin. Haughty and confident, she smiled. Behind her, Mrs. Barton-Forbes gulped the dregs of her highball. Lady Alfreda twined her fur piece nervously between her fingers.

"Oh no you don't, Gloria. Not this time." Richard Senior shrugged off Bea and Meredith, squared his shoulders and started pushing his way toward Lady Simpson.

So did Richard, stumbling winded and rumpled out of the crowd near the opposite fence, just in time to see Meredith jump piggyback on their father's shoulders to stop him. He didn't look where he was headed, he didn't need to, he saw it in Susan's pinched face, felt the first tiny rip in his head.

"There he is!" his grandmother shrilled. "Richard, you ninny! Come here this instant!"

"Richard, darling!" Alfreda crooned.

He ignored them, shoved his way toward Susan and felt another rip down the back of his head. He set his jaw and kept moving, felt another tear shiver down his spine.

Susan saw him as he pushed a photographer roughly out of his way. One lapel of his dovetailed morning coat was torn, his vest was missing all its buttons, but he'd never looked more handsome as he smiled and opened his arms.

This was her fantasy, her second-best dream come true. She and Banner and Richard in the winner's circle. Susan ran into his arms.

Awash in lavender and Susan's tears, Richard clung to her and felt the rip slide like a zipper back up his spine. He was whole, he was loved, he belonged.

"Dickie!" His mother screeched.

"Dickie?" Richard Senior roared. "How dare that woman call *my* son Dickie!"

Lifting his head from Susan's hair, Richard stared, openmouthed, at his father who was still struggling to peel Meredith off his back. *My son.* He'd said it almost proudly.

"Makes you sound like an obscene little watch fob." Richard Senior turned his head to look at his son. "Has she always called you that?"

Richard grinned. "Except when she's mad at me. Then she calls me Richard."

"I see," he said grimly, hooking his hands under Meredith's knees so she wouldn't slide off his back. "Well she won't anymore."

Her hat long gone, her blond hair drooping out of its chignon in wisps around her face, Meredith gave a cowboy whoop and clamped her hands on her father's shoulders as he bore down on Lady Simpson. Over Susan's head, Richard saw Loren beating his Stetson at people to clear a path through the crowd for his father and Bea.

"Hurry, darling," he said, lacing his fingers through Susan's. "We don't want to miss the battle of the titans."

Susan didn't feel ugly and gauche anymore, she felt gorgeous, despite the angry, jealous glare on Lady Alfreda's face and the hateful gleam in Lady Simpson's eyes as she lifted her veil. She felt happier than she'd ever been in her whole life. Even in her dreams.

Though she was vastly outnumbered, Lady Simpson held her ground as Richard Senior swooped down on her. Hooking one arm around his neck, Meredith lifted the other and waggled her fingers at Richard's mother. Then, because she thought no one else could see her, she stuck out her tongue.

Richard grinned, his mother's gaze narrowed and Alfreda burst dramatically into affronted tears. He couldn't imagine, let alone remember, what he'd ever seen in her.

"I'll thank you, madam," Richard Senior said icily, "never to call *my* son Dickie again."

This time Richard knew for sure he hadn't imagined the inflection his father gave the pronoun. He stopped beside him and drew Susan into the circle of his right arm.

"He's my son, too," Lady Simpson retorted imperiously, "and I'm not leaving here without him."

"Yes you are, Mother," Richard told her firmly. "Right now, before you make a scene."

"*Me* make a scene?" Lady Simpson swung a dangerously glittering gaze on him. "I don't have some silly little moppet with knobby knees clinging to my back or some blowsy redhead stuck to my side like we're joined at the hip."

The insult stung Susan, but only for the half second it took Richard to tighten his arm on her shoulders. She caught Lady Alfreda's eye as she raised her left hand and let the amethyst flashing on her finger speak for her. Lady Alfreda gave a wail and threw herself on Mrs. Barton-Forbes's neck.

"Knobby knees!" Meredith cried, taking a swing at Lady Simpson over Richard Senior's right shoulder.

The punch missed as he took a quick step back, but Bea didn't. Her face as pink as her ruined suit, she wormed through the crowd pressing around them and let fly with her handbag. It caught Lady Simpson on the shoulder and sent her stumbling backward into her mother and Lady Alfreda.

They fell in a heap of stockinged legs and flying hats, Mrs. Barton-Forbes drunk enough and Alfreda young and limber enough not to be hurt. No one in the crowd straining around them seemed to notice. Gentle Bea, who Richard had never heard so much as raise her voice, stood legs spread over Lady Simpson with her purse cocked for a second swing.

"Way to go, Mom!" Meredith crowed.

"Beatrice!" Richard Senior shouted. He was trying his damnedest to sound shocked, Richard thought, but the corners of his mouth were twitching.

"Now Bea—" Loren said soothingly, easing up to her like a skittish horse.

"Back off," Bea snapped at her brother-in-law. "I've had twenty-five years of this bitch and her threats and tantrums. Get up, Gloria. Get up so I can belt you again."

Lady Simpson struggled up on her hands, knees together, ankles turned. She puffed at a lock of dark hair in her eyes and flung a sizzling look at Bea.

"Mummy, do something!" she screeched furiously.

Flat on her back behind her, Mrs. Barton-Forbes wrenched her cane out from under the sobbing Lady Alfreda and shoved it at her daughter. "Here."

"Richard," Susan said, tugging urgently on his untorn lapel.

"I'm going," he said, reluctantly, and gave her shoulders a quick squeeze before stepping between Bea and his mother.

"Well finally," Lady Simpson huffed indignantly, taking the hand he offered her and struggling ungracefully to her feet on one broken two-inch heel. "How *could* you just stand there and let this dowdy creature humiliate me in public!"

"Dowdy creature!" Bea wound up with her purse again, then yelped furiously as Loren locked his arms around her, lifted her off her feet and swung her away.

"That dowdy creature," Richard said to his mother, "is more a mother to me than you ever thought of being. The knobby-kneed moppet is my sister—"

"*Step*sister," Lady Simpson cut in frostily.

"My *sister*," Richard repeated fiercely. "The redhead is my fiancée, and God help you if you ever call her anything but Susan ever again."

"How *dare you* speak to me in that tone of voice!" Lady Simpson raised her right hand to slap him.

"Behave yourself, Mother, or you won't get an invitation to the wedding." Richard caught her wrist and looked past her at Mrs. Barton-Forbes. "Go home, Gram," he told her. "Go to hell," he said to a white-faced, grass-stained Alfreda.

Then he kissed his mother's cheek, dropped her hand and walked back to Susan. Not a single screech followed him.

From the corner of his eye he saw Meredith press her cheek to Richard Senior's, saw his father lift one arm and sweep Bea against him. Over her mink-trimmed pillbox hat, he saw Loren grin and wink at him as he plunked his Stetson back on his head. Last he saw Susan and smiled. She smiled back at him, her eyes shining.

The balloon in Richard's chest swelled one last time, then burst forever. Somehow, somewhere in his rotten, miserable life he'd done at least one thing right—he'd made Susan Cade love him.

Wrapping his arms around her, Richard closed his eyes and inhaled her wondrous lavender scent. When he opened them, he saw Luke leading High Brow away, her head drooping in defeat.

"Aren't you going to kiss me?" Susan murmured.

"In a minute," he said, catching her hand. "First I have to see a man about a horse. Hey, Luke!"

He turned toward Richard and Susan and lifted his sunglasses. His black eyes were green today.

"I'm in the market for a horse," Richard told him. "I'll give you eleven thousand, three hundred and sixty eight dollars for this loser."

High Brow snorted, affronted, and threw up her head. Richard slipped her a wink.

Luke pursed his lips and pretended to consider it. But the twinkle in his eyes as he caught the pleading look on Meredith's face gave him away.

"I'm outnumbered and I know it," he said with a grin. "Tell you what, Four Eyes, old buddy. If you can ride her, you can have her."

"A wise choice, Lumpy old chum. Gimme a leg up."

"Richard," Susan said, catching his arm. "I don't want High Brow. I want you."

Right here, right now. Richard read it in the amethyst shimmer in her eyes, as clearly as he'd murmured it to her three nights ago in the foaling barn.

"Don't worry." He dropped a kiss on her nose. "I know what I'm doing." Confidently Richard stepped forward as Luke adjusted the stirrups, then cupped his hands for Richard's foot and bounced him up into the saddle.

"Oh my God!"

Susan heard Lady Simpson's scream and looked over her shoulder in time to see her faint dead away into Lady Alfreda's hands. She tried, but couldn't feel sorry for her, then grinned up at Richard who was doing a masterful job of controlling the prancing, dancing High Brow.

"Never mind, slugger," she said to him with a laugh. "I guess you do know what you're doing."

"Sometimes I get lucky." Richard grinned and held a hand down to her.

Unmindful of the throng still milling around them, Susan caught the hem of her silk skirt and gave it a rip, first halfway up her left thigh, then halfway up her right. A few brave men wolf-whistled until Richard shot meaningful glares in their direction. Kicking off her heels, Susan slid her foot into the stirrup Richard freed for her, caught his hand and swung herself onto High Brow's back behind him.

The filly shifted a bit but took their weight. Slipping her arms around Richard's waist, Susan laid her cheek against his back and smiled down at her father. He blew her a kiss as High Brow moved off at a trot toward her barn.

The crowd gave way for her and the show she put on, prancing and tossing her head. She'd lost this race but there'd be others. Under the red-and-white silks of Roundhouse Stables, Susan decided, choosing not to lay claim to her gift horse until High Brow had run her last race with the wind. Half a lifetime of friendship deserved that much.

Outside her barn, High Brow came to an automatic halt. Susan slid first to the ground, Richard after her, catching the filly's reins in his hands as Susan opened the barn door.

High Brow's stablemates turned their heads and whinnied to her, stretching their necks over their half doors. They could sense a loser, and withdrew one by one into their stalls as Susan and Richard led her down the corridor. Her head drooped lower, her ears went flat against her head, until she reached the stall she shared with Satan.

The old pony was there to greet her, barely tall enough to poke his nose over the half door and touch his muzzle to hers. He whickered to her from deep in his chest. High Brow snuffled mournfully. Satan snuffled and shook his head.

Richard could have tuned into the link, but didn't. Just smiled at Susan over the filly's withers as she lifted her head, stamped a hoof and pricked up her ears. Satan gave a satisfied snort.

While Susan stripped off High Brow's saddle and bridle, Richard gathered a halter and a cooling sheet from a nearby tack room. A tack room with a cot for the grooms, a stack of quilted winter blankets on a shelf, and a lock on the door.

He made a note of the cot and the lock and headed back to High Brow's stall, where her groom had appeared to take charge. The filly twitched her withers as Richard tossed the sheet over her, held still while her groom fastened her halter and clipped on a lead rope. As he led High Brow outside to walk her and cool her down, she swung her head around to look at Richard. He could've sworn she winked at him.

"Come with me," Susan said, catching his hand and leading him into the tack room.

Richard went with a smile on his face, spread a blanket on the cot, then took Susan into his arms. He kissed her while he shut and locked the door, while he undressed her and himself and lowered her onto the cot underneath him.

She opened for him but he didn't take her, just worshipped all her lush, sweet curves and the dark, secret places of her body with his mouth. Her eyes were a deep, misty amethyst when he came inside her, his senses filled with her heady lavender scent and the smell of clean, fresh straw.

"I didn't invite my mother here," Richard finally remembered to tell her. "She and Gram and Alfreda have been hunting me for the last week. I don't want you to think I had anything to do—"

"Never mind, darling," Susan murmured, pressing her fingertips to his lips. "I know."

"Please, Susan." Richard caught her hand and kissed it. "Just this once would you let me tell you?"

A Note from Lynn Michaels

I love horses and fairy tales, so writing *Second Sight* was double fun for me. I love horses because they're beautiful—I cried the day Secretariat died—and fairy tales because they have happy endings. That's also why I love to write romance.

Every good fairy tale has magic. In this story, it's Susan's ability to talk to horses, something I wish I could do. I like to think there are people who really can.

I chose to update *The Ugly Duckling* because it's a story with universal appeal. We can all relate to feeling ugly on the inside, no matter how we look on the outside. We all dream of waking up some day to discover we've become swans. Some of us are still waiting. Others, like Richard, have been a swan all along. It just took him longer to realize it. And Susan's love to convince him.

Take 4 bestselling love stories FREE

Plus get a FREE surprise gift!

Special Limited-time Offer

Mail to Harlequin Reader Service®

3010 Walden Avenue
P.O. Box 1867
Buffalo, N.Y. 14269-1867

YES! Please send me 4 free Harlequin Temptation® novels and my free surprise gift. Then send me 4 brand-new novels every month, which I will receive before they appear in bookstores. Bill me at the low price of $2.44 each plus 25¢ delivery and applicable sales tax, if any.* That's the complete price and—compared to the cover prices of $2.99 each—quite a bargain! I understand that accepting the books and gift places me under no obligation ever to buy any books. I can always return a shipment and cancel at any time. Even if I never buy another book from Harlequin, the 4 free books and the surprise gift are mine to keep forever.

142 BPA AJHR

Name	(PLEASE PRINT)	
Address	Apt. No.	
City	State	Zip

This offer is limited to one order per household and not valid to present Harlequin Temptation® subscribers. *Terms and prices are subject to change without notice. Sales tax applicable in N.Y.

UTEMP-93R

©1990 Harlequin Enterprises Limited

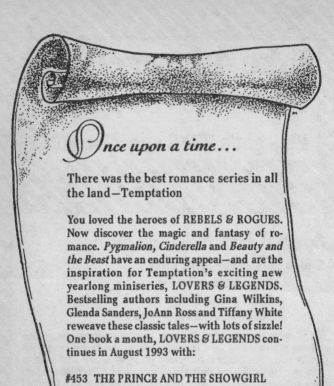

𝒪nce upon a time…

There was the best romance series in all the land—Temptation

You loved the heroes of REBELS & ROGUES. Now discover the magic and fantasy of romance. _Pygmalion, Cinderella_ and _Beauty and the Beast_ have an enduring appeal—and are the inspiration for Temptation's exciting new yearlong miniseries, LOVERS & LEGENDS. Bestselling authors including Gina Wilkins, Glenda Sanders, JoAnn Ross and Tiffany White reweave these classic tales—with lots of sizzle! One book a month, LOVERS & LEGENDS continues in August 1993 with:

#453 THE PRINCE AND THE SHOWGIRL
JoAnn Ross
(Cinderella)

Live the fantasy...

LL8